DETECTIVE & MYSTERY

BKM Mil 11/13/99 D

x

Salvage for the Saint

W9-BUD-893

F.2.

Leslie Charteris'

Salvage for the Saint

Original teleplay by
John Kruse

Adapted by
Peter Bloxsom

G.K.HALL &CO.
Boston, Massachusetts
1988

The villains and situations in this book
are entirely imaginary and bear no actual
relation to any real person or happening.

Copyright © 1983 by Leslie Charteris.

Published in Large Print by arrangement with
John Farquharson Limited.

G.K. Hall Large Print Book Series.

Set in 16 pt Plantin.

Library of Congress Cataloging in Publication Data

Charteris, Leslie, 1907–
   [Salvage for the Saint]
   Leslie Charteris' Salvage for the Saint / original teleplay by John
   Kruse ; developed by Peter Bloxsom.
       p.   cm.—(G.K. Hall large print book series)
   (Nightingale series)
   ISBN 0-8161-4631-4
   1. Large type books.   I. Kruse, John.   II. Bloxsom, Peter.
   III. Title.   IV. Title: Salvage for the Saint.
[PR6005.H348S47 1988]
823'.912—dc19   88—16292

Forenote

After some thought, I am making a brief intrusion here, in preference to a footnote later.

This offspring of the successive talents of John Kruse and Peter Bloxsom, whom attentive readers will recognise as seasoned veterans of the latter-day genre of Saint adventures, is linked with just one feature unique among these semi-pastiches with which I have tried to beguile you over the last few otiose years.

Besides performing my usual rôle of meddler with the original television script (in which I frankly had a lot less authority than I had in revising this book which is now based on it) I had on this occasion the rare pleasure of spending a couple of weeks with the crew shooting in the south of France, making myself fractionally useful in suggesting and scouting locations and so forth. I even had the privilege of making a short but necessary voyage on the luxury yacht chartered at awful expense to play the part of the *Phoenix*—an experience in sampling how a real millionaire can live which I shall never forget.

But to make the memory even more special, by being on the spot I was able to con the amiable director into letting me walk through a tiny and totally unimportant scene. Thereby consigning myself, for once only, to video immortality.

No prizes are offered for spotting me in this extraordinary appearance. But when the TV Movie is re-run—as it assuredly will be—this Forenote might just give you a hint of what to watch for.

Or maybe not.

St Jean — Cap Ferrat
October 1982   L.C.

Contents

I: How Simon Templar anticipated a Lady's Plea, and Charles Tatenor went Astray.

—1——

Like so many of Simon Templar's hair-raising adventures, it began with a beautiful girl and led him to a merry-go-round of battle and murder and sudden death, and there was booty by the ton.

All of which, from Simon Templar's point of view, was very much as it should have been. Those were the established ingredients of his life, and he could hardly remember a time when he would have wanted it otherwise.

But the ingredients never came together in the same way twice: it was never exactly the mixture as before. And that was a blessed bounty, a sublimely serendipitous piece of good organisation for which Simon Templar —who was also known as the Saint—never ceased to offer up thanks to whatever wise providence might have been responsible. To him the exhilarating wine of adventure had it own numberless subtleties of region and

1

vintage, so that it always tasted fresh and bracing on his palate and made every escapade different and new.

This one was to take him from the Isle of Wight, that Mecca of yachtsmen and sandcastle-builders off the south coast of England, and down through France to the Mediterranean on a freewheeling chase across land and sea, and under the sea, and into the past . . .

He was finishing off some vigorous bedtime calisthenics with a toothbrush when he heard the soft but insistent knocking on the door of his Cowes hotel room.

He shrugged into his dressing gown, a positively shrieking green foulard effort, and made his way to the door. The knocking stopped briefly; then it re-started. The Saint paused, with his hand hovering over the doorknob.

His immediate impulse, the impulse of his temperament, was to open up without preamble and confront the late visitor. But one result of his years of notoriety was that it was never close season on Saints these days, and there were some hard against-the-grain compromises he had had to make for the sake of staying alive, which he considered an important priority. One of these reluctant compromises was the habit of challenging people who knocked on his door—especially people who knocked on his door late at night.

He spoke, aiming a short sharp question through the wood.

"Who is it?"

He would have been the first to agree that it wasn't a startlingly original utterance. But it did have a certain workmanlike quality to it. It was a practical and utilitarian piece of dialogue answering perfectly to the needs of the moment.

The reply came in a vibrantly confidential whisper that thrilled its way back to him after the most fractional of hesitations.

"Mata Hari."

It was good enough for the Saint. He opened the door—and saw at once that she was as gratifyingly beautiful as all uninvited late callers ought to be.

For her part, the first thing that hit her eye was his eye-searing robe; and it was a measure of her self-control that she confined her reaction to a single blink.

"Come right in—sunshine," he invited, and led the way.

She puzzled a moment over the endearment as she followed him into the room, which in point of strict accuracy wasn't a room only but a suite, and wasn't even a suite only but nothing less than the most luxurious and expensive suite in the hotel. Simon Templar was sometimes inclined to extravagance, though he used an economical gesture now to indicate a chair.

"Your drink will be—let me guess—a gin and tonic. Am I right?"

Even as he spoke he was already at work at the compact cabinet, mixing the drink with an unhurried adroitness that few men could have matched without years of professional practice. By the time she nodded her agreement with his selection the ice was already tinkling into the glass; and it seemed only a bare few seconds later that the Saint was lounging back in a chair facing her with his own choice of alcoholic refreshment in his hand.

He studied her gravely for a few moments.

"Mata Hari," he said, by way of explaining his greeting. "Either from my encyclopaedic knowledge of eastern languages or else because I came across the fact in a magazine somewhere, I happen to know that the words come from the Malay. Where

4

English uses the crude and unimaginative monosyllable 'sun', the Malays say 'mata hari'—literally, it means 'eye of the day'."

"Oh," she said, smiling. "How poetically oriental."

"And in your case, I'd say, quite appropriate. I'll bet you bring a lot of sunshine to a lot of old men's dreams simply by strolling along by the harbour wall." He paused, eyeing her reflectively. "That is, when you're not too busy with the binoculars."

She laughed, softly and with a kind of lilting warmth.

Of course, she'd known all along that he must have been aware of her. Four days ago he had come to the island bringing a lithe zestful fitness and a little leashed tiger of a powerboat, and in those four days she had hardly missed a single chance of watching him in action.

The Saint, who did many things superlatively well, was tipped as an eminently watchable challenger in tomorrow's big race to Penzance, the first since the war; and she, it seemed, had decided that he was just as watchable during the run-up period. Like most of the other serious competitors, he and his navigator had got there a few days in advance for preparatory fine-tuning of both boat and men. It was a time to get oriented to the surroundings and the race atmosphere, too—and maybe to suss out the competition a little . . .

Just as the girl, for reasons of her own, had been sussing out Simon Templar.

At close quarters she had watched discreetly, cool and elegant behind inscrutable dark glasses on the hotel or Yacht Club terrace or on a bench near the Southampton ferry just along from where his boat was moored. At long range she'd resorted to the binoculars, which ostensibly followed her husband's conspicuous and massively powered yellow cruiser but panned a frequent deviation, sweeping along the Solent skyline till they found, and locked on, the creamy bow wave and flashing red hull of Simon Templar's *Privateer*.

She had studied his bronze six feet two inches of superb physical condition and noted the relaxed yet alert way he carried that steel-sprung muscular frame. Her gaze had lingered on the chiselled piratical features and tried to fathom the elusive light of something like mockery that danced in his reckless blue eyes. She had measured objectively the supreme confidence and competence of his fluid movements, the style and elan and sheer exuberance with which he did even the simplest thing.

And she had approved.

Of course, she had known him before, in the legend. He was the incomparable modern swashbuckling hero, the twentieth century's brightest buccaneer, the preposterously handsome knight errant whose exploits around the world had made more headlines than some Hollywood starlets had had affairs. His reputation, in short, was as familiar to her as to any of a hundred million of so newspaper readers—to say nothing of Charteris devotees—from Los Angeles to Liverpool, from Tasmania to Togoland.

But now she had seen him for herself, and she had approved.

And he would have had to be at least moderately unobservant—which he was not—to have been unaware of her thorough scrutiny.

"You noticed, then?" she said, because it was something to say.

The Saint didn't reply at once—or not in words.

He allowed his glance to flit over her— rapidly, but deliberately and pointedly. The travel of that impudent gaze began at her red-gold hair, which was styled in a simple but perfect upsweep; it went on past a face that neither needed nor apparently received much help from artifice but which could still have launched a thousand powerboats; it took in a series of feminine curves which are best described as ripe, correctly positioned, and expensively coutured; and it continued to her ankles, whose sculptural virtues would have defeated the pens of much more highly paid chroniclers than this.

And having completed that comprehensive downward voyage, the Saint's shameless gaze embarked on the return.

An inspection as frank as that could easily have seemed rude, but coming from him it somehow didn't. He had a feel for these things, seeming to know by effortless instinct how to flatter a civilised woman without running too much risk of offending her.

As his eyes swept back up to her face, completing a survey the whole of which had taken a bare few seconds, she met his gaze again calmly without flinching or reddening.

He said simply:

"Yes, I noticed you. I'm sure you know just how beautiful you are."

It could have been a barbed compliment, but wasn't. He said it without any imputa-

8

tion of vanity on her part or any embarrassment for himself. He made it sound the most natural remark in the world; and he went on in the same candid way.

"Let's face it, being inconspicuous isn't your strong suit. And neither is modesty mine. Sure, I saw you giving me the once-over . . . and the twice-over. And I'd've been as flattered as hell except for one thing."

She raised an eyebrow in query. She was still smiling.

"A certain notoriety," he said. "One of whose effects is to make strangers stare a bit from time to time. Even beautiful redheads whom I might be only too pleased to imagine were interested in me simply as a man. Your inspection was certainly rather more persistent than most, though. So I had to reckon with the possibility that you'd be around knocking on my door before long. But I also had to reconcile myself to the fact that, if you did come, it almost certainly wouldn't be on account of my irresistible manly torso . . . Mrs Tatenor."

He threw out the name lightly, knowing it would be no surprise to her that he knew it.

"It's Arabella," she said quickly. "But of

course you've seen me with Charles." There was a mischievous twinkle in her eye as she went on. "In fact, I seem to remember that you were close enough to our party in the clubhouse yesterday to have seen that I was drinking . . . gin and tonic."

The Saint sighed.

"You have no faith in my omniscience," he said sadly.

She eyed the tough-looking broad-shouldered figure swathed in dazzling green who lounged before her, and her lips curved in an enigmatic half-smile.

"No. Only in your—more human powers. And I'll have you know that your irresistible manly torso does have something to do with that."

He raised a shocked eyebrow.

"You mean you've decided I'm man enough for—for whatever it is you have in mind?"

"Even that Noel Coward outfit can't disguise the capabilities of the Saint," she said lightly.

It was an agreeable enough game, he thought, this fencing with *double entendres*. But it wasn't getting them very far or fast along the road she'd started on when she'd decided to call on him.

10

"By the way, how did you know my room number?" he asked casually.

She eyed him in amusement.

"I asked the desk clerk when I came in. Isn't that what you'd have done?"

The Saint took a thoughtful pull at his drink.

"Probably. But I'm not a married lady with a reputation to look after."

"Reputation phooey!" She made a face. "I don't give a fig for that sort of notion."

Her convention-defying stance struck a chord, and Simon grinned.

"The hell with desk clerks," he agreed. "Anyway, you're here, having made quite a preliminary investment in reconnaissance."

He waited patiently. She drank deeply, taking her time.

"Yes. *You* have a reputation—a particular reputation—for involving yourself in all sorts of troubles. Sometimes other people's troubles."

He waited while she downed most of the remaining half of her drink. Then she continued, still giving an impression of some reluctance to come to the point.

"And I know that when you do get involved in something it's usually because you've sniffed out some nasty bit of business for yourself—or some specimen of human vermin you just can't resist smacking on the snout. But occasionally when you weigh into the affray, it's because you've been *asked*."

Simon Templar took a long pull from his own drink—he had some catching up to do—and regarded her soberly. (They were weakish drinks.) He studied her relaxed posture, her calm face, her big bright untroubled eyes.

"And you're asking?" he queried.

"Certainly," she said. "After all, I understand you specialise in damsels in distress."

—2——

The Saint smiled inwardly as well as outwardly. It looked as if he had one very out-of-the-ordinary lady here, and he was glad he had the opportunity to get to know her better.

"Of course I do," he answered. "Doesn't every self-respecting redblooded knight errant? But . . . ." The upward displacement of one dark eyebrow was minute, but sufficient to suggest a polite skepticism that was barely distinguishable from complete open-mindedness. "But . . . *are* you in distress?"

She wrung her hands helplessly and batted her eyelashes at him nineteen to the dozen.

"Is that better?"

They both laughed; and then she said seriously:

"Simon, I may not be as demonstratively in distress as some of your classic damsels. Technically you might even say I'm not in distress at all. Certainly I don't think I'm in any kind of personal danger." Here she looked wistful, almost as if she would have rather enjoyed being in personal danger. "All of which may seem to disqualify me as a true dyed-in-the-wool d in d. And all of which is part of the reason why it's taken me four days to make up my mind to come and see you."

"And the rest of the reason?"

"The first part of the rest of the reason is that I'm an independent-type girl and I don't like asking for help. And the rest of the reason is—well, call it natural skepticism."

"You mean when it comes to the providential arrival of a rescuing knight on a white charger that looks more like a red powerboat?"

She gave a thumbs-up sign.

"You got it in one. Where rescuing knights are concerned, I'm a total unbeliever. Or was. I'd heard and read all about the famous Saint, of course. But frankly I thought you were just too good to be true."

She paused, draining non-existent dregs from her glass.

"But anyhow," she continued, "I hesitated to bother you at a time when you're—well—" She spread her hands in a vague gesture that seemed to indicate satisfactorily the island and the circumstances of his being there.

"On vacation?" he supplied.

"Something of the sort, I guess. Only I didn't think you daredevil freelance buccaneer types went in for fixed periods of work and leisure as such."

"We don't," he agreed. "Or at any rate this one doesn't. For me the work's a kind of vacation in itself most of the time, so it doesn't break my heart when an earmarked vacation turns into work, as it looks like doing now."

He was trying gently to coax her to get to the point, but he knew enough about her already to be sure that she would continue to take her time. It came, he suspected, from a kind of careful-stepping delicacy in her character; and that was something he could respect, even if it meant his bedtime was thereby delayed a little further.

He said nothing for a few moments while he repeated his legerdemain with the glasses; and then he regarded her silently for a few moments more, with a level blue gaze in which there was a shifting light she had seen before, a light that was elusively mocking and quixotic and challenging all at the same time.

He said: "So you took a good gander at me and decided that the stainless purity of my character spoke for itself—eventually?"

"I decided," she answered slowly and deliberately, "that against all probability, everything I'd ever heard and read about you was true—or at least, all the good things—and that there's no comparative stranger I'd be readier to trust."

The Saint blinked.

"That was quite a speech," he said. "Thanks. I'm flattered, I really am . . . Of course, if you got to know me better, disillusion would soon set in. You'd find I have to cut my toenails and wash my socks just like ordinary mortals. On occasions I burp, and I have even been—"

"Oh, give me every time a man who really knows how to burp!" she purred, clapping her hands in beautifully judged over-enthusiasm.

And she laughed again with the same rich encompassing warmth as before, a warmth that was peculiarly feminine and flattering in itself. It somehow blended intimacy and reserve and mystery and promise; and it made the Saint study her some more.

He put her age somewhere between twenty-five and thirty. Those were, from a male point of view, the best years for certain types of women, and in Simon Templar's connoisseur opinion she was certainly one such type. She was the type whose features in rather earlier youth might well have seemed a little underformed, a shade on the doughy side. But as the years swung by and bone structure began to assert itself, as the faces of her contemporaries took on an edge of hardness hers would simply have lost its excess softness to emerge as the example of perfectly sculptured beauty it had now become.

Yes, a woman like that came into her own between twenty-five and thirty. Especially if she'd managed to keep a healthy skin, unraddled by the clogging attentions of the multitudinous offerings of chemico-cosmetic quackery on whose efficacy the greater part of credulous womankind have been induced to pin such a pathetic faith.

Arabella Tatenor had certainly managed the miracle of dermal preservation, though whether she'd done so by shunning face goo or in spite of using the stuff Simon couldn't tell. Her skin was smooth and clear with a healthy pink glow. She had the eyes to go with it, too, translucent blue like the Saint's own; and above them was the spun copper sweep of her hair. He wondered about her colouring; maybe there was a strong Irish, or at any rate western fringe Celtic, contingent somewhere in her pedigree. But it must have been some way back because there was no trace of Irish in her speech. He'd known at once that she was American, or at least predominantly American. It wasn't so much from any strongly marked accent as from her choice of words. She'd said "that sort of notion", which had a transatlantic ring, and she'd referred to the "desk clerk" where a speaker of pure British English would probably have said "receptionist", and of course she'd said "vacation" rather than "holiday". The Saint was sensitive to such minor differences of idiom even though his own international background meant that he had himself long since adopted a style of speech which freely mixed the usages of Britain and the US. He noticed, for instance, that she pronounced "asked" in the American way, and "clerk" to rhyme with "lurk."

Yet at the same time there was a good deal of *English* English in her pronunciation. It had hardly any of the strident nasalisation of much American speech. Boston was the first likely area that came to mind, but to the Saint's ear she sounded still more English than that.

"Fitzpatrick was my name before I married," she remarked, latching on to his thought with near-clairvoyant accuracy. "A solid New England family and filthy rich. When I was fourteen my parents sent me over here to raise the tone of Cheltenham Ladies' College. And then on to Oxford."

"Where you took a brilliant double first in Byzantine history and molecular physics while ruining the academic dedication of countless slavering male students," hazarded the Saint.

"Where I got bored after two terms of Eng. Lit," she corrected, "and took off into the wild blue yonder."

"Much to Daddy's disgust, no doubt."

18

"Much."

"And then?"

"I travelled the world. Bumming around, mostly, I guess you might call it. Having a ball. Until the money ran out. I have some expensive tastes, and after Oxford—well, the milk of parental generosity just kind of dried up."

He grinned as he made another open appraisal of her expensively tailored figure.

"I imagine your style in bumming around might be comparable to Gloria Vanderbilt."

She fielded the grin and returned it to the accompaniment of a reproachfully levelled forefinger and the same mischievous twinkle in her eyes as he had seen there before.

"Don't you make a mistake," she warned, "of thinking you have me all figured out and labelled and docketed. Because let me assure you, you haven't, Mister Saint, not by a long chalk."

The Saint erected a momentary barricade of arms and elbows in front of his head in mock terror at her stern finger-wagging warning.

"OK," he said penitently. "Maybe I'll buy that. And I'll consider myself roundly rebuked. After all, you did take four days over me. I suppose I ought to wait at least as long before making up my mind about you . . . But there's one confident guess I'll risk."

"And what's that?"

"That the problem that's prompted you to call on me—after due examination of my credentials—isn't entirely unconnected with a certain bullet-bonced Gallic leech—"

"—that's attached itself to my connubial other half," she cut in, smoothly finishing the sentence in almost exactly the words the Saint would have used.

He laughed, and behind the laughter was a passing inward delight which he couldn't have expressed, though it had to do with two people's thoughts being oddly tuneable to the same pitch, and with the rarity of that in the real world.

"You speak my kinda language, blue-eyes," he Bogarted. "We must be using the same scriptwriter."

"Well, he's good and he's cheap, isn't he?" she Bacalled huskily. "And why should you have all the best lines? . . . But coming back to the Gallic leech"—she had reverted to the blended tones of Oxford and New England—"of course, you could hardly have missed him. You've probably heard his name

too. Fournier. Maurice Fournier. Mean anything to you?"

"The name—no. But that phizog. That
does ring some sort of bell."

He had already racked his brain repeatedly in a vain struggle to recall where he
had seen that unprepossessing face before.
Almost the first out-of-key phenomenon to
catch his attention among the varied mani-
festations of boating and boat-watching humanity in and around Cowes that week had
been the short thick-set shaven-headed man
who seemed to have no higher or more engrossing purpose in life than that of keeping
himself glued limpet-like to a point approximately three inches from the elbow of
Charles Tatenor.

Tatenor himself lived on the island.
Squarely built, greying, fiftyish, he was a
sophisticate of British sporting circles, and
the faster and more expensive the sport the
better he liked it. Powerboat racing fitted
very well; Tatenor's was one of the leading
names around the world, and even if Simon
Templar had his own ideas about who was
going to win the two-hundred-mile race
along the coast to Penzance, it was certain
that Tatenor was the favourite in most people's books.

Which fact made it all the more surprising to everybody else that he had suddenly decided to ditch his experienced navigator Taffy Hughes in favour of this newcomer who not only seemed to have difficulty telling the sharp end from the blunt end of a boat but gave every appearance of turning pale green as soon as he came within spitting distance of the ocean—incidentally an appropriate expression, as Fournier spat frequently.

Hughes—Simon had commiserated with him over a drink—was as mystified as anyone. Tatenor had simply told him that Fournier was an old friend from way back, and that for old times' sake he had agreed to his friend's joining him in the race. But in explaining this to Hughes, Tatenor had worn a face of acetic sourness that seemed at variance, in Hughes's alcoholically emphasised opinion, with the professed friendly spirit behind the gesture. And from his own observation the Saint had to agree that Tatenor's way of eyeing his long-lost chum was anything but chummy.

But where Tatenor went Fournier went. When Tatenor went aboard his boat, though it might only be to work on the engines, Fournier went along. When Tatenor drank in the Royal Yachtsmen's Club—usually without Arabella in attendance—Fournier drank too. And when Tatenor went home to his extravagant hillside home above Egypt Point, just outside the town, that dogged French shadow went with him. It was as if the two men were joined by an invisible chain.

A part of the Saint's mind was working again at the puzzle of trying to match the Frenchman's fishy features against something obscurely out of focus in his memory; and he wondered if some circumstantial detail might give him the clue he needed.

"Just how long has Fournier been on the scene?" he asked Arabella.

"Six days," she told him. "He just turned up at the house one night. Our place is just along the road from here. Well, when this Fournier thing showed up that evening"—she wrinkled her nose in distaste—"Charles was obviously more than a tiny bit flabbergasted, and none too delighted either. It was over twelve years since they'd met. Anyway, he stayed to dinner—Mrs Cloonan's a miracle-worker, she can always cope with a guest at the drop of a hat—and next morning there he was again at breakfast. That's when Charles told me Fournier'd be staying till after the race, and then the two of them'd be going off on business together for a few days. And ever since, Fournier's hardly let Charles out of his sight. Except today."

"What happened today?"

"Charles gave him the slip for a few hours, after the scrutineers had finished their main stint this afternoon. Charles took the boat out on his own, and he didn't come back till the evening."

The Saint digested the information thoughtfully.

"I suppose he didn't say where he'd been?"

"No. Just 'out in the boat'. I could see Fournier was livid when he'd discovered Charles had gone, but he calmed down later."

"When he saw that Charles had come back?"

"That's the way I read it."

"Hmmm. Any idea what this joint business of theirs might be?"

'To do with his investments or something like that, I guess. I didn't ask." She shrugged. "I enjoy helping to spend Charles's money, but I've never quizzed him about how he makes it. I only know he doesn't actually have to *do* much . . . But

Simon, now that you're on the case—and you *are* on the case, aren't you?" She broke off and eyed him hopefully, and then went straight on without waiting for an answer: "—now that you're on the case there's something I should tell you. Charles and I, we're getting a divorce soon."

"I shan't pretend to be surprised," Simon told her quietly. "I've seen the two of you together, and you don't exactly radiate marital harmony and contentment, if I may say so. But I suppose this has nothing directly to do with Fournier's intrusion into the household?"

"I'm not citing him as co-respondent, if that's what you mean!" She laughed, but this time it was a rather more brittle laughter. "No, there are plenty enough contenders for that honour already. And save your sympathy, Simon," she added quickly. "I'm at least half to blame. I guess the whole thing was a mistake from the start."

"How long has it been?" he asked gently.

"Four years."

"And he's—twice your age?"

"He was, then. But that's not really the problem. I liked him okay. But I liked his money too, in about equal degree."

Simon expostulated mildly.

"Oh, come on. Aren't you being a bit hard on yourself? You're making yourself sound like a cold-hearted little gold-digger, while I'm sure you're not."

"Well . . . maybe not so cold-hearted." She looked at him for what seemed a long time; one pair of blue eyes candidly searching another. "But as I've told you, I have expensive tastes. I like money and I like men with a lot of it. Charles fitted the bill. It wasn't enough though."

She smiled wryly, and for a little while her eyes were clouded with an unreadable wistfulness. Then the Saint said:

"What about his reasons for getting in tow with you?"

She laughed the brittle laugh again.

"They were as shallow as mine. Basically, he wanted, if you'll forgive me, an attractive wife, something reasonably decorative to be seen on his arm at Brands Hatch and Le Mans and Cowes. But Charles'll always be a womaniser, anyhow. So, all things considered, I'm for getting out of the game and cutting my losses."

"Or is it taking your winnings?" Simon suggested mildly.

"Ouch," she winced. "I guess I asked for that. But yes, I'll admit that as far as money's concerned, I do want to get out with something to the good. Though whether you call it winnings or earnings is debatable. Now, to return to Fournier. First, there's something about him I don't like. But it's more than personal dislike. He's got some sort of hold over Charles. It's as if Charles were knuckling under, and I don't know why. Maybe Fournier's blackmailing him—something in his past. And Charles's past is something I know practically nothing about. He's never talked about it, certainly not in any detail. Anyhow he's certainly rattled. And I'm concerned. First in a human, or even if you like in a wifely way. I really don't want anything bad to happen to him. And secondly, and you may think this is the bigger component in my concern, I have a financial stake in Charles and I want to look after it."

"I think I get the picture," Simon said, not without sympathy. "You're afraid hubby may decide to do a bunk to escape the clutches of comrade Fournier, and you're worried that if he does vamoose he may well get the bright idea of arranging for all the family shekels to vanish along with him, before you've had a chance to get your hands on your share."

27

"You put it with real delicacy," she said sarcastically. "But that about sums it up. As I told you, I know next to nothing about his money, *our* money, or even how or where he keeps it. As things stand I get a regular allowance, but if Charles does cut and run before the divorce hearing, well, if I know him, he'll take every brass farthing with him. Which will mean phut to my chances of a settlement. Before long I'd probably have to take a—a *job*."

She spoke the final word with a shudder.

"An obscene idea, I agree," said the Saint.

"So," she concluded. "That's it. What I'd like you to do is to keep an eye on things. Maybe find out what's going on between Fournier and Charles."

Simon maintained a neutral uncommitted manner.

"And if they go off together after the race as planned, I suppose you want me to follow them? Or if Charles makes a run for it, you want me to follow him?"

"That's it."

She eyed him hopefully, but his gaze was studiously inscrutable.

"If not for me, then for yourself," she urged, trying another tack. "Fournier, now—he's pretty obviously, I should say, one of those human excrescences you love to squash . . ."

Again the hopeful glance. "Isn't he?" she asked.

The Saint's inscrutability was still as politely impenetrable.

"He's a slug of a man," she declared firmly.

The bantering lift of a dark eyebrow gave nothing away.

"A disgusting parasitical creature," she continued. "A wart on the nose of humanity! A carbuncle on its neck! A lump of—"

The Saint held up a restraining hand.

"The trouble with you," he said severely, "is that you've been reading too much of the stuff that fellow Charteris writes about me. But that's by the way. On this occasion I happen to agree with you. If appearances are anything to go by, Fournier is indubitably a pluke of the first water."

"Quite," she agreed, and then reverted to her other tack before he could recover his breath. "And what's more, a fair settlement in the divorce court is my just right. And the court won't even get a look in if Charles decamps with the stocks and bonds and whatnot. What say you, Simon? Will you help?"

The Saint laughed, and the two pairs of candid blue eyes met again.

"I'm on the case," he said. "To tell you the truth, I've been on it since yesterday."

—3—

In the ten minutes before she left the hotel, he told her what he had achieved so far.

There wasn't much to tell, since his limited labours had yet to bear fruit.

It was on the previous day that he had stood Taffy Hughes a couple of consolatory beers, and it was then, immediately after that talk with Tatenor's supplanted race colleague, that the Saint had made up his mind to upgrade his casual interest in the pushy French interloper into something more actively investigative.

He had begun there and then.

All he had to go on was the vague feeling that he'd seen Fournier's ugly mug somewhere before. That suggested an obvious starting point, and the Saint refused to let its obviousness put him off starting there. He ran the *Privateer* a few miles along the island's coast to Ryde, a bigger and less specialised resort where the business he had in mind could be transacted more discreetly. From a locally recommended photographic dealer there he hired some valuable hardware, and then he cruised back to Cowes Harbour and took his navigator and co-driver, Vic Cullen, aboard for the afternoon's practice session—the final one before the race.

They checked over the engines and equipment, made a couple of adjustments, and then churned their way out across the mild swell for a routine of offshore speed runs and practice starts. Little more than half an hour went by before they saw the big yellow splodge that was Tatenor's boat, the *Candecour*, detach itself from the quay and cream its way in turn across Cowes Roads into the Solent proper to begin some limbering manoeuvres of its own. And then, still keeping a cautious distance between the boats, the Saint had proceeded to indulge himself with some long-range portrait photography.

They were too far out, he judged, for this interesting recreation to be spotted even through Arabella Tatenor's binoculars, assuming her to be deploying them as previously; and in any case the Saint's photographic efforts were completed in a few swift seconds.

The telephoto equipment he had borrowed enabled him to get some candid if unsteady mug shots of the hairless Frenchman, who was just then looking even more woeful than usual owing to the sensation of complete inadequacy that had engulfed his digestive organs from the very first seconds of the *Candecour*'s motion.

The Saint had returned the photographic paraphernalia that same evening, and its estimable and conveniently incurious owner had next obliged him with some speedy developing and printing. Several among the most rather blurred shots of Fournier were passably recognisable; and these the Saint had sent, with a brief covering note, to a useful unofficial contact of his in London's sprawlingly complex web of officialdom.

Knowing that corruptible Civil Servant to be both unrushable and thorough, the Saint was resigned to waiting several days for a report which, when it did arrive, would certainly be as informative as it could be made. If there was anything to be had on Fournier, the gentleman Simon Templar knew as Beaky would assuredly pass it on.

The Saint was content meanwhile to concentrate his mind on the race.

It was just three hours away when he woke up on the morning after Arabella Tatenor's late visit. From his window he had a view north across the water to the mainland. He saw at once that the sea was a good bit rougher than it had been; the day was bright with some patches of blue up aloft but the sky was in continual turmoil as huge grey clouds raced before a boisterous wind.

It was one of those clear fresh gusty days which occur sometimes in England at any season; days when everything stands out with such a perfectly focused clarity that it seems almost as if the wind itself had scoured the land and sea clean of all their fuzzier outlines. The mainland at its closest point was five miles away but seemed a good deal nearer. Looking across the arms of the Solent to Southampton water the Saint could distinctly make out the figures of the individual passengers on the decks of a big P & O liner, greyish white with one ochre funnel, that was just turning east on its way out to the open sea. He watched idly for a minute or two as it ploughed into the waves with a ponderous slow-motion plunging progress, like a great anaemic whale. Beyond lay the quiet stretch of wooded coast from Hill Head up to Warsash and Bursledon, inaccessible except on foot or from the water. From his viewpoint on the island it usually appeared as a smudged mass of dark green, but now he could have counted off the thousands of trees one by one.

The English summer may not be quite as mythical as some visitors have concluded, but its reputation for unpredictability is largely deserved. Like an inconsiderate annual houseguest, it can't be relied upon to put in an appearance on schedule, or even to show up at all; and when it does appear it may arrive without notice and depart the scene just as abruptly. By these elastic standards this year's summer had been a good one, the Saint observed to himself. The warmth had lasted pretty well without interruption right through from mid-June until this late August morning, when the abrupt-departure habit had manifested itself in temperature a good twelve to fifteen degrees down on the previous day's.

The wind was shifting about skittishly from moment to moment but blowing mostly from the west: which meant that the powerboats on their mainly westerly course would be headed directly into it.

All of which meterological observation the Saint summed up to himself in this way: navigation straight forward, thanks to the visibility, but in every other way a rough, tough race.

He girded up his figurative loins to meet this prognostication by consuming a leisurely and substantial hotel breakfast. As he munched his way imperturbably through grapefruit, wheatflakes, a buttered Finnan haddock that overhung the plate, and a mountain of toast, washed down with a pint or so of coffee, he looked forward to the exertion to come.

The diet wasn't the recipe for obesity that it might have been. He expected to burn it all up very quickly in the race. He expected to use a lot of energy in the eight or ten hours it might take him to win it. He knew that besides the drain of continued concentration on achieving every bit of non-suicidal speed the conditions might allow, there would be the constant exertion of riding the boat's bucking motion so as to stay approximately upright and functional for all the time. He knew that he and his partner would need to draw liberally on their fitness, and he fully expected to see some of the competition drop out sooner or later for want to that same fitness.

He had dressed for the race simply and practically in tough canvas trousers and oiled-wool sweater. As he strolled out of the hotel entrance, he met a shorter strong-looking man who was similarly clad but with the addition of a dark wollen beret on his close-cropped head.

"OK, Vic?" The Saint grinned, clapped his navigator on the shoulder, and fell into step beside him.

"Positively rarin' to go, Soimon."

An answering grin split Vic's broad canny face, which had the high colour of a man who had spent most of his life in the open air, summer and winter.

"Tin't 'alf gointa be rough roide, though," he added with a glance at the sky.

"Looks like it," the Saint agreed. "But there's one consolation in that. If it's uncomfortable for us, think how uncomfortable it's going to be for at least one member of the Tatenor team. And if that slows 'em down a fraction, I don't suppose you and I'll be the first to complain."

"Reck'n not," Vic agreed, with a broad cheerful wink and a single oblique sweep of the head that was an expressive gesture half-way between an affirmative nod and a negative shake. "But ut's a fast boat they've got there, arl roight . . . a moighty fast boat."

He paused as they turned to walk the last hundred yards along the harbour wall past most of the opposition to the *Privateer*'s mooring. "Reck'n we can beat 'em though," he added thoughtfully.

"I reckon we can," said the Saint.

Vic Cullen was a boatbuilder from Bursledon, across the Solent. After thirty years' working with boats, on and off the water, there wasn't much anybody could teach him on the subject. He had built the *Privateer* virtually single-handed to a design he and Simon had worked out together. His only help with the work had come from the Saint himself in the odd intervals of his exigent adventures elsewhere.

The teams of scrutineers were busy with their final inspections, and the salt breeze carried a low babble of voices from the waiting competitors, punctuated intermittently by the raucously variegated notes of motors starting up. Beneath that man-made and evanescent hubbub was something powerful and eternal—the rhythmical slap and swell of the sea. Even here against the harbour wall its motion was noticeably stronger than it had been in the last few days, and as Simon and Vic neared the short jetty where the *Privateer* was moored they could see her scarlet hull bobbing up and down impatiently, and hear the stretched creaking of wet rope as she tugged at her moorings.

"Strainin' at the leash, look," Vic said with pride; and the Saint nodded and smiled, sharing that same pride.

"Scrutineers should be with us in a few minutes," he said. "She'll just have to contain herself till they've done."

This was her first race; and it was for racing above all that this trim compact boat had been built. She was every inch a beauty; but it was the beauty of a spare and functional design. Every line of that sleek hull, from the futuristically cutaway stern to the streamlined cockpit canopy and steeply raked bow, had been calculated for speed. She was a thoroughbred racing machine, a slim-line twenty-two-foot lightweight with a modest five litres of engine and with the irreducible minimum of fittings and frivolities allowable within the race rules, which in those days were not over-elaborate.

Those days were, roughly speaking, the beginning of the modern revivalist era of powerboating competition, before the introduction of more rigid systems of boat classification and qualification. Less than midway through the twentieth century, the sport had been enthusiastically rediscovered after a lengthy neglect, and its free-for-all freshness attracted a colourfully wide range of hopefuls.

The Cowes-to-Penzance race that year was a typical result; but the record books will be found to be mysteriously obscure on the subject if not altogether blank. The fact is, nevertheless, that there were thirty-six entrants in all: thirty-six assorted boats receiving the scrutineer's final check on that windy August morning.

The degree of assortedness was astonishing. Simon Templar had cast an incredulous eye over many of them, and had decided that the owners' choice of names for their boats offered a rough and ready indication of their chances.

Those blazoned with the most intimidating appellations—*Thundershark*, *Tornado*, *Hell for Leather* and the like—mostly turned out to be the tiny, infinitely hopeful outboarders. At the other extreme were the half dozen big thirty-five- and forty-footers representing the brute force approach: plenty of bulk and up to a thousand horses of petrol or diesel power to blast it across the waves. For some reason, maybe connected with having a faulty sense of humour, the proud owners of these jumbo-size entries tended to have given them coy names like *Buckaboo*, entered by Sammy Topwith of motor racing fame, *Big Bouncie*, a fancied US contender, and *Skimmie*, the great hope of the Aussies.

Somewhere in among this litter of the inept and the overpowered was the gold of real racing, boats built for the job and handled by men who knew what it took and had what it took. The names in this group had a romantic flavour that suggested their clean graceful lines: *Dolphin II*, *Red Marlin*, *Silver Lady*, the crack Italian boat *Bellissima*—and Simon Templar's *Privateer*.

Moored near the *Privateer* was Charles Tatenor's massive yellow boat, the *Candecour*. With her overall length of thirty-eight feet and her six-hundred horsepower twin Rolls-Royce diesel engines she fell decidedly into the brute-force category, although the name was an exception to the general trend, and had no obvious derivation that the Saint could see. She was a conversion rather than a purpose-built job, but in this case the work had been carefully and professionally done even though most of the luxury fittings had been preserved. Tatenor had even added to the ostentation, by having the external trim finished off with a series of intricately carved mahogany panels and an ornate figurehead in the shape of an eagle; all of which gave the *Candecour* an outward air of rococo excess that belied its brisk performance on the water.

Tatenor himself was standing a few yards away on the quayside with Fournier. Each of the two men was wearing a one-piece waterproof suit and carrying a bright orange crash helmet.

Though Simon had exchanged the odd word with Tatenor within the ambit of this and previous races, he preferred to dislike him cordially at a distance. But Tatenor caught his eye now, and flicked a depreciatory finger at the *Privateer's* scarlet hull.

"I do hope she holds up for you," he called across.

"You'll be able to follow her progress for yourself, and without turning your head," replied the Saint with even politeness.

Tatenor laughed hollowly, exposing teeth of perfect porcelain translucence whose shade matched the white of his hair and contrasted with the deep tan of his handsome weather-beaten features.

"I suggest you might care to check the boiler in that thing before we start," he brayed, flicking another dismissive finger in the *Privateer*'s direction and chuckling at his own remark.

"And you," retorted the Saint good-humouredly, "had better lash down the Chippendale and be prepared to jettison a couple of footmen when the going gets tough."

"Boiler!" Vic exploded softly to Simon as Tatenor turned away with a frozen smile on his large brown face. "We'll show *you* somethin', Mister lah-de-dah Tatenor!"

Simon felt vaguely uncomfortable himself with Tatenor's speech, for some reason he couldn't quite pin down. It was a discomfort that was something more than simple dislike of the parodied form of English articulation inflicted on the rest of us by certain representatives of the old-guard sporting gent brigade, of which Tatenor seemed to be almost a founder officer. It was decidedly something more than that; it was the kind of discomfort, the kind of nebulous puzzlement, which the Saint had felt before in all manner of circumstances when something was micrometrically off-key and his senses were busy delivering messages to his understanding which that partly instinct-driven system refused to accept as making a wholly convincing picture. When Simon Templar felt this way he could be sure there was something behind it which with luck and persistence he would presently ferret out from his subconscious. But that would happen in its own time, and for the moment he had the race to think about and no intention of actively worrying away at a nagging disquiet about Charles Tatenor's speech.

But then something reached his ears which was all the more thought-provoking for being so wholly unexpected.

He heard Charles Tatenor speaking to Fournier in perfect French.

4

Even though the two had turned away before Tatenor spoke, the Saint's acute hearing picked up the sentence clearly. He heard Tatenor translate, for Fournier's benefit, the last flippant remark of his own about the Chippendale and the footmen.

Whether Fournier grasped the satirical point at once is doubtful—judging from the corrugations of puzzlement that appeared on his unprepossessing brow—but incidental. The noteworthy thing to Simon Templar, himself an exceptional linguist and fluent French speaker, was Tatenor's perfect assurance in the language. His apparently effortless impromptu translation would have been hard to better, but so would his pronunciation, accent, and—the most difficult—intonation. To the Saint's ear, which was assuredly no mean ear at all as ears for that sort of thing went, Tatenor's French was as indistinguishable from the French of an educated Frenchman as his English was from the English of an educated Briton.

And that reflection provoked a line of thought to which the Saint was to come back again and again, during the race and after.

During and after. Especially after. Because the race ended, for Simon Templar, in an unexpected way, and for Charles Tatenor more surprisingly still . . .

It began, however, in the way that was usual for the times: with a rolling start. Powerboats are only semi-controllable at sub-planing speeds when a big group of them

44

are frothing along in a turmoil of contending washes, and to let them spin and jockey for the best positions as at the start of a race for yachts would be asking for trouble. Discipline was therefore imposed on the scene in the form of a start boat with the function of pacing the competitors up to the line for a rolling start, so that they would all cross the line more or less together and at the same speed.

The Saint manoeuvred the *Privateer* into her drawn lane position towards the outside of the muster area, about a mile and a quarter behind the line, with the start boat on the extreme outside, farthest from the Cowes shore and the assembled thousands who had gathered to watch what little of the race a landbound spectator could hope to see. Four minutes before the off, with a final blip of motors, the start boat set off for the line, rapidly reaching the planned speed of just over fifteen knots. As a concession to traditionalists a starting-gun was fired from the start boat just as she crossed the line; but few of the competitors could have heard it above the noise of their engines. The trick was to keep fractionally astern of the start boat—any boat crossing the line ahead of it would be disqualified.

Simon Templar kept fractionally astern of it.

He heard the gun, faintly, as they crossed the line, and then he eased the throttle open to about two-thirds maximum to get the boat up on the plane, as the jargon has it. After a minute or so he opened the throttle a little wider to raise the speed experimentally as far as he dared in that decidedly assertive sea.

The Saint looked around, through the heavy spray the *Privateer* was throwing up.

He was lying second. Two or three boat lengths ahead, away on their port, was the Italian entry *Bellissima*. It seemed to be leaping from one wave crest to the next, its propellers sometimes rising right up out of the sea. Each time it took off, the ocean seemed to fall away vertiginously beneath it—and every time it landed it hit the water with a tremendous smack and was momentarily all but obscured from sight by the rising spume. And the Saint and Vic were only too well aware that exactly the same thing was happening to the *Privateer*, and that to an observer outside the boat the repeated impacts probably seemed equally likely to smash it to smithereens at any moment.

The equations of propulsion and drag in a high-speed motor boat are finely balanced; every day presents its own parameters of wave rhythm and current and wind resistance. The first rule of thumb you learnt was that the less the boat was in actual contact with the water the faster it would go. But all propulsion had to be achieved through the water: airscrews or rockets would disqualify the craft as a boat. So you were dependent on your propellers and it was important that they stayed under the water as much as possible to keep the propulsion going continuously. Too little up on the plane and you followed a switchback course over the peaks and down into the troughs of the waves, with a heavy drag of water resistance on the hull. Too much up on the plane to minimise that drag, and you risked losing more than you gained as your screws clawed frequently at empty air.

And that, to the Saint's eyes, was what was happening now to the Italian boat. While it had pulled ahead of him in the first minutes, probably by getting more rapidly and less cautiously up to its optimum speed for the conditions, it had now overshot the mark and he was very slowly gaining on it. But his judgment told him that if anything the

47

Privateer herself was maybe erring fractionally in the same direction, and now he slackened off the throttle an almost imperceptible notch.

Vic nodded approval and agreement, then touched the Saint's arm and pointed astern, to their nearer port. Perhaps half a dozen lengths behind was the *Candecour;* and it was plain to them both that the big boat was gaining on them.

Simon sighed.

"I'm afraid we're going to have to let him past."

He knew there was no help for it. A couple of minutes after they had inched past the *Bellissima,* they were in turn overtaken by the *Candecour,* some fifty yards on their port. The yellow-helmeted figure at the wheel, which must have been Tatenor, raised an arm as they went inexorably and infuriatingly by. He waved, though without any shadow of the gaiety that might have been conveyed by an orthodox reciprocation of the upraised hand. Tatenor's wave was a single one-shot extension of the arm from an upright to a forward position. It was almost a salute, but with an element of gloating finality in it which seemed in some way chilling.

"Snotty bastard!" Vic snorted with feeling.

But Vic knew, with the same seamanlike feel for the interaction of boat and waves and weather as Simon Templar's own, that there was nothing to be done. They were skimming over the water as fast as the *Privateer* could skim in those conditions, in that direction, on that day; and it so happened that the *Candecour* was travelling faster. In fact, though they hated to admit it, Tatenor's boat was optimising that difficult equation better—for the moment—than their own.

For the moment . . . Those, the Saint told himself with set determination, were the operative words. For the moment, the *Candecour's* great weight and bulk might suit the conditions, but much as it depressed him to see that yellow stern drawing steadily away in front, the race was a long way from won yet. For the moment, they still had the north coast of the island off their port side. But soon they would clear its western extremity, marked by the Needles, a familiar landmark of jagged rocks that stuck out of the sea like the angular protuberances of some giant sea monster's submerged body. Beyond this point the boats would encounter a completely different series of currents. Wave amplitude would probably change too, and they would be battling into a still stronger headwind than they already faced. And then . . . there was more than a chance that the *Privateer* would come into her own.

Simon glanced around. The *Bellissima* had fallen steadily farther behind, and the next boat was so far back that it was impossible to hazard even a guess at which one it might be.

The Saint's mouth set in a grim fighting line as the Needles came into view. This was the stuff of life to Simon Templar: to be thrown on his mettle, to be seemingly outrun, for the moment, but to have reserves and resources of his own as well as all the glorious imponderables of time and chance to rely on.

"We'll catch him," he said, with quiet certitude.

And there came a time, not many minutes later, when the *Candecour* ceased to open up her lead any farther from the four hundred yards it had become. And not many minutes after that, it became apparent that the gap was very slowly but steadily closing.

They were more than an hour into the race now, and with their progress westward the crowds lining the shores on both sides of the water had dwindled until now they were confined to a few loose knots of people on the beaches of the minor holiday resorts in Christchurch Bay to their starboard. Milton on Sea, then Barton with its crumbling rufous cliffs, then Highcliffe, then Mudeford, guarding the northern side of the narrow entrance to Christchurch Harbour. That entrance was actually invisible from the Saint's viewpoint, being almost completely closed off by the sandy promontory known as Hengistbury Head, which curled around from the south west like a beckoning finger.

They were about two hundred and fifty yards astern of the *Candecour* when it happened. They were battling now into a moderate sea, which means a lot of battling for small boats, and as they rose and fell with the waves they frequently lost sight of the *Candecour* for a few seconds at a time.

It was after one such occlusion that the yellow boat suddenly veered off right and began cutting obliquely across the *Privateer*'s course.

"What the blue blazes—?" Vic followed up the mild oath with a more fluent and earthy profanity, and they watched in astonishment as the *Candecour* tore off towards

51

the shore, without any visible slackening of speed.

The Saint was trying to hold a steady line on the boat with his binoculars. He shook his head in puzzlement.

"At that rate she'll plough straight into the Head . . . The funny thing is, she's holding a dead-straight line, yet as far as I can see, there's no one standing up to steer her. Which is a more than mildly interesting way to tackle a race."

The *Privateer* had now passed the other boat's point of eccentric departure, so that they now had her almost directly to starboard. As far as the needs of continuing to manage the *Privateer* in that demanding sea allowed, they watched the *Candecour*, with a fascination that afterwards seemed like foreknowledge of what must inevitably happen.

"Throttle must be jammed open," said Vic softly. And then, when it seemed certain that big yellow boat must plough into the beach at any second, they made another abrupt turn, or half-turn, to starboard.

"She's missed the Head," said the Saint, "but she's going straight for the rocks."

The *Candecour* never did slow down . . . until those rocks compelled a deceleration as abrupt as it was spectacular. The engine note was terminated by a splintering impact. Then a moment's suspension of time. Then it came. A white-orange flash, and two or three seconds later the sound of the blast.

After a moment's thought, Simon Templar eased off the throttle slightly, spun the wheel hard right, and pointed the *Privateer* at the blazing inferno that had been Charles Tatenor's boat.

II: How Arabella began a Journey, and Simon went Beachcombing.

——1——

The Coroner cleared his throat sympathetically.

"Mrs Tatenor," he said tentatively, but with the determined firmness of a Pillar of the Establishment who knows that he must Do his Duty, however painful, "there still seems to be some mystery concerning the identity of your husband's co-driver."

Arabella Tatenor nodded. She had already had more than enough of the meticulous, punctilious coroner. Her expression, if it conveyed anything, conveyed mild boredom.

She was dressed befittingly in black; but her skirt and blouse, for all their sombre colour, had clearly been cut without the slightest intention of concealing the shape of what they enclosed. And what they enclosed while draped around Arabella Tatenor had plenty of shape.

As for the shape she was in generally, on taking the stand a few minutes before in the crowded Ryde courtroom she had raised a filmy black veil to reveal features only a shade or two paler than they had been before the events of five days ago.

The Coroner was a large bony man with a well-scrubbed and barbered look. His black hair was shaved to an exaggerated short-back-and-sides respectability that gave him something of the look of an SS officer. He wore a dark-grey pinstriped suit, a white shirt with old-fashioned detachable collar starched and pressed to a celluloid shine, and a spotted tie done up in a tight little knot.

"The name you gave the police," he went on. "Maurice Fournier. No one of that name has been traced. If you could possibly recall something that might—"

"No, there's nothing," cut in Arabella rather brusquely. "He said his name was Fournier. That's all I know."

The Coroner hesitated.

"But he was a guest in your house for a week or more."

"He was my husband's guest. I'd never met him before. And when I did meet him I took an instant dislike to him."

The Coroner pursed his lips and brought two sets of five fingertips carefully together.

"Well, perhaps you can assist us by saying whether you formed the impression that Fournier was his true name?"

"No, I formed no impression about that. I had no reason to question whether it was his true name."

"And what is your impression in retrospect, in view of the fact that the French authorities say that no Maurice Fournier is known to them?"

Arabella shrugged, making no particular effort to hide her impatience.

"Authorities can be wrong," she told him. "And anyway he could easily have been Swiss or Belgian or something. But I really don't see that his name matters. He, and my husband, are both dead."

The Coroner winced visibly at the nakedness of her words, as if he would have liked to substitute something more bland and bloodless like "passed on" or "deceased". Simon Templar, who was also in court, smiled at the thought of the interior battle that the Coroner must have been waging with himself at that juncture—a battle between, on the one hand, the legal ego, which hates to let anyone get away with robbing it of the initiative in argument as she had just done, and on the other the well-brought-up conservative gentleman whose sympathy for a newly widowed woman makes him a bottomless fount of indulgent tolerance.

The gentleman won on points, even if his fount did emerge as unmistakably non-bottomless. Its visible bottom took the form of a restrained concession to the legal ego; the Coroner swallowed hard—a species of exertion that caused his protuberant Adam's apple to twitch the knot of the spotted tie—and said with forced pleasantness:

"You must allow me to be the judge of what matters in this case, Mrs Tatenor. But I realise how distressing all this must be for you. I am sure you have the sympathy and good wishes of everyone present in the court, and I hope we shall now be able to conclude this inquiry quickly. You may stand down now."

She made a movement that just barely feinted at being a hint of a half-bow that she'd thought better of, and went back to her seat, which was next to the Saint's in the second row of the block reserved for witnesses and members of the public.

In the front row of the same block sat the press-men, taking up their full allocation; on the Saint's other hand sat Vic Cullen, and every other seat in the small Ryde courtroom was occupied too. Among the assembled faces Simon recognised at least half a dozen of the other race drivers; the rest were mostly holidaymakers who happened to be on the island at the time and who for reasons of their own considered a Coroner's Inquest a good afternoon's entertainment.

The Saint had half-turned in his seat to survey the spectators with casual interest, and his gaze had just stopped thoughtfully at two vaguely familiar-looking men whom he couldn't for the moment place in either the boat-racing or the holidaymaking group—both were overdressed and one was unusually fat, with a drooping moustache— when the Coroner spoke again.

"Mr Simon Templar—will you take the stand now, please?"

The Saint stood up, took the stand, and went through the usual initiation ritual.

The Coroner eyed him with evident distrust. The Saint resisted the urge to stick his tongue out, and contented himself with returning the Coroner's cold stare in kind.

"You are the man they call the Saint?" asked the Coroner.

"The same."

The Coroner sniffed, and made a nervous adjustment to the knot of the spotted tie which left it in exactly the same position as before.

"Mr Templar, your reputation is well known. You have often been described as a common criminal, and I have to say that you are by no means the sort of witness with whom I should have preferred to have to deal in this court."

The Saint smiled. He didn't intend losing sight of the seriousness of the occasion, but the opportunity was too good to miss.

"That's quite all right," he replied generously. "To be frank, you're by no means my favourite type of coroner, either."

There was a brief eruption of laughter, started by a couple of reporters. The Coroner glared at them and went three shades pinker. The Adam's apple and spotted tie wiggled as he struggled to get control of himself.

"However," he went on, heroically abstaining from comment on the Saint's riposte, "I am told that your knowledge of power-boating matters is sound, Mr Templar, and I understand that you and your co-driver Mr . . . ah . . . Cullen were the first on the scene after the explosion."

"That is correct," agreed the Saint in a businesslike tone.

"I have here your eyewitness report, taken by the police at the time." The Coroner indicated the document in front of him. "Perhaps you will help us by expanding on one or two points."

"If I can," said the Saint.

"One thing puzzles me in particular. Mr Tatenor's boat suddenly changed course and began heading for the beach at . . ."—the Coroner peered at the papers—". . . Hengistbury Head. You and Mr Cullen could hardly help being aware of this sudden turn, since the boat cut right across your own course."

"Correct."

The Coroner leaned forward.

"But having changed course in that abrupt manner, the boat then continued in the new direction, still heading straight for the shore, for a distance of approximately half a mile?"

"As you say—approximately."

"Does that not seem to you a little odd, Mr Templar?"

It seemed to the Saint decidedly odd, but he hadn't the slightest conscience about pretending otherwise to the Coroner.

"Not in the least odd," he said in a tone of conviction.

"But how would you explain it?"

60

"What seems to me the most likely explanation," Simon lied, picking his words with care, "is that the boat hit a big wave, and that as a result both men lost their footing, hit their heads and were knocked cold."

"Leaving no one at the wheel?"

"That's right. It could easily happen. It was a very choppy sea."

"But with nobody at the wheel," persisted the Coroner, "wouldn't you have expected the boat to follow a rather erratic course, instead of travelling a good half mile or more in a straight line?"

It was a question the Saint had expected and one that had, somehow, to be answered. He took a deep breath.

"I suggest," he said with a magnificent airy confidence that made everything seem much simpler than it was in his real thoughts on the matter, "that one of those unconscious bodies became slumped or wedged against the wheel just after they hit the big wave. The rudder would probably have found its approximate straight-ahead position very quickly in any case, on the principle of least resistance, and the wheel would have gone back with it, rather like the wheels of a car straighten up and take the steering wheel back after you round a bend. If one of the two men then fell against the *Candecour*'s wheel, as I think must have happened, that would have kept the boat on a roughly straight-ahead course."

"Thank you, Mr Templar."

There was a begrudging note in the Coroner's voice but he continued to nod sagely as if to imply that of course he had seen all this for himself and now had come to the really difficult question. He posed it triumphantly.

"Yet, just before the impact, according to your evidence, the boat made *another* abrupt turn, and then *once again* straightened up." The Coroner paused for effect. "You're not seriously suggesting, Mr Templar, that the whole exact and rather unusual sequence of events which you have postulated was repeated?"

"No," said the Saint with patient civility, "I'm not suggesting that. The explanation's far simpler. When the *Candecour* got near the head, she hit the rip tide—that's all."

"Ah, the rip tide," said the Coroner, little enlightened.

"At the right time," the Saint explained with a briskly authoritative note in his voice, "which means during about the first two hours of the ebb, there's a very sharply demarcated rip tide off the Head, moving almost parallel to the coast at up to twenty-five knots. I think it's pretty clear that the rip was enough to deflect the *Candecour* and turn her through maybe another thirty or forty degrees, but not to stop her. So she hit the rocks farther along."

On this specific point Simon Templar's confidence was genuine. The rip tide was fact—the *Privateer* herself having had to battle obliquely across it to get to the blazing wreckage—and he was as sure as he could reasonably be that the *Candecour*'s final turn had been consistent with the rip tide's likely effect on her runaway progress.

Otherwise, however, he was sure of nothing except that, somewhere, things were not entirely as they seemed . . . After the searing inferno that had been the *Candecour* had more or less burned itself out, two big lumps of something resembling charcoal had been recovered from the drifting debris. Each had the vestigial metal frame of a crash helmet all but fused to its charred skull. It was fortunate, from the Saint's angle, that the Press had observed their normal reticence in the matter of giving specific details of the bodies. In particular they had said nothing about the crash helmets. Nor, it seemed, had the Coroner been reminded of them by anything in the papers. Simon's own original eyewitness statement had foresightedly avoided direct reference to them—because even then he had been thinking ahead to the inquest. For when Simon Templar was on a project—and he regarded himself as still very much on this project, even if its terms of reference had altered somewhat since Arabella's nocturnal visit—the last thing he wanted was great flat-footed policemen stamping about the scene of the crime, or interesting questions to cramp his own style.

Therefore he had kept the crash helmets out of the discussion. If they had been brought into it they might have made the Coroner and jury just that important shade more likely to doubt his airy explanation of the crash. For two men to be knocked cold at the same time is by no means beyond the bounds of credibility, especially when the proposition is put by someone as blandly authoritative and seemingly convinced by it as he had taken care to appear. But a double knock-out when both men's heads were protected by purpose-made helmets? Any reasonable member of the jury, and certainly the critical Coroner, might have balked at that . . . if the facts had been brought together in that way, which they had not.

The Saint had got away with it. He had calculated his performance to satisfy the all-important Coroner and jury, even though in the process as a boat expert he might have taken a nose-dive in the esteem of some of his racing colleagues.

The case was all over in another half-hour. Technical witnesses appeared, were questioned mechanically, gave their evidence after their own styles, and were duly dismissed. There was an RAF officer from the safety launch which had accompanied the competitors in mid-field and had made an early attempt to put out the fire; a marine fire expert who wrapped up the obvious— that the boat had exploded—in egregious jargon; a lugubrious forensic medical expert who confirmed that the bodies were too burnt for identification; and a dentist who, with a good deal of hedging and qualification and puffing and blowing said that the teeth were no help either.

The jury brought in their expected verdict of accidental death on Charles Tatenor and "one known as" Maurice Fournier; and Tatenor's widow sighed with visible relief and left the court on Simon Templar's arm.

They climbed into the powerful silver Aston Martin he had hired on the island, and talked about nothing in particular as the Saint's effortless touch threaded the car through the twists and turns of the island's narrow roads as if he had known and driven them for years.

And then abruptly Arabella asked the question he had known she would have to ask.

"Simon—you don't think Charles could have committed suicide, do you? And killed Fournier at the same time?"

The Saint shook his head.

"No, I don't," he told her firmly. "And neither do you. I don't think either of us can seriously see Charles as a suicide. And if he'd wanted to get rid of Fournier there are a dozen ways he could have done it without blowing himself up at the same time." He glanced sideways at her thoughtful profile. "Right?"

"Right," she agreed.

It was plain enough to Simon that she saw no real reason to doubt seriously that Tatenor's death had been an accident. A spectacular accident maybe, and coming at a time when there was pressure on him, but an accident just the same. After all, powerboat racing had its risks—that was part of the appeal of the sport to men like Charles Tatenor.

"I'll be sticking around for a couple of days," Simon told her as he dropped her outside the opulent Victorian grange above Egypt Point which she now had all to herself—except for Mrs Cloonan.

The plump motherly housekeeper, whom Simon had met briefly a couple of times during the past few days, was staying on with Arabella, and she appeared now in the doorway and waved as he drove off.

During the two or three days for which he planned to stay on, the Saint meant to be busy. He was waiting now with supercharged curiosity to see whether his friend Beaky would come up with anything interesting on Fournier, but he had some investigating of a more active kind to pursue in the meantime. After that . . . well, Arabella was resilient and would be more or less back on an even keel in a couple of days; and if the Saint's suspicions were borne out he might have something more than mildly interesting to tell her—something which, had he been able and willing to tell it at the inquest, would have been enough to set the stuffy Coroner's larynx to a positive frenzy of twitching.

The Saint smiled at the thought. Coroners are coroners and Saints are Saints, and never the twain . . . But at the back of his mind, when he remembered the inquest, something nagged; a small insistent voice which prattled in no very intelligible language of an undigested thought, some loose end left, some fragment of information his brain so far hadn't had time to process.

It was much later that he remembered.

He had been glancing around the courtroom idly examining the audience, when his eye had fallen on those two overdressed, foreign-looking men sitting together, one of them very fat and the other lizard-like. And the detail which in retrospect seemed to him especially interesting—the detail he had noted in passing at the time but had so far not returned to ponder on—was the exact quality of the reaction he had seen in the fat man's flabby bandit face when the Coroner had announced the name Simon Templar.

—2——————————————————

Arabella Tatenor extended an irritable brown leg from the pink wickerworks swing seat and pushed away the tiny white toy poodle that was positioning itself neurotically to spring into her lap for the fifth time in as many minutes.

She wagged a reproving finger at the highly strung overbred travesty of doggyhood.

"Don't be a bore, now, Phaideaux."

The wretched dog jittered and quivered, fixing its mistress with beseeching black button eyes. A little bell fixed to its collar tinkled annoyingly with its every movement, and next to this dangled a solid silver plate that confirmed the spelling of its name—pronounced, of course, exactly like "Fido." It was her not-so-dear departed husband who had thought up this piece of linguistic tomfoolery and tongue-in-cheek snobbery, and Arabella had once found it amusing enough.

But at this moment her thoughts were elsewhere than on the dog; and neither were they directly concerned with the departed.

More with what the departed had left behind.

Opposite Arabella sat a very large man who had somehow shoe-horned himself into a very small wrought-iron chair. He was large in as many dimensions as the chair was small, with florid features and an unruly mop of greying hair. He was wearing a rather crumpled blue suit and had an attaché case balanced precariously on his knees, with a stack of papers balanced still more precariously on top of the case.

This was Richard Brightly—Brightly Senior of Brightly, Brightly and Smallbody, Solicitors, and he had just told Arabella, twice, slowly, that Charles Tatenor had died broke.

"I'm sorry." She blinked groggily. "Charles was *what?*"

"Broke." Brightly riffled through the stack of papers. "Your husband was broke. You are broke. I'm sorry."

"Broke? Don't be ridiculous." She reached impatiently for the papers. "What are those?"

Brightly held them out to her.

"Unpaid bills."

Arabella jerked back her hand as if the papers were red hot. Her face had taken on an expression of mingled amazement and indignation which suggested that she was beginning to take the idea seriously. She opened her mouth a couple of times to say something, then gave up the struggle. Sensing its opportunity, the dog scampered up into her lap.

70

"Quite," Brightly said. "But you see, my dear, there really is a butcher, a baker, a—"

"Wait a minute, now," Arabella said in a bloodless voice. She put the dog down, less gently than before, and stared hard at the solicitor. "Are you saying just . . . broke? I mean, you don't really mean *broke*-type broke?"

Brightly inclined his head apologetically.

"But . . . !" Arabella spluttered. She gestured around her. "Does this look broke to you?"

"It looks rented."

"Rented? *Rented?*" she repeated unbelievingly; and then dully: "Rented."

"I'm afraid so, my dear. Did Charles really never tell you? But this house, the cars, practically everyth—"

"Of course he told me," she interrupted mechanically. "Charles told me everything . . . What the hell do you mean, *rented?*"

The dog risked another assault on her lap. She put it down with a brisk "Get lost, Phaideaux," and addressed the solicitor again.

"Charles had income, though. I know he did."

Brightly nodded.

"He paid his debts twice a year, because

71

twice a year he managed to come up with a large sum of cash. From somewhere."

"Somewhere?" She shook a murderous finger at the dog, which was preparing to launch itself at her again. "Where?"

"He'd never say, and I could never learn."

"But . . . this is absolutely ridiculous—"

Perhaps fortunately, her frustration, bewilderment and anger were interrupted at that moment by the arrival of a filled tea-tray, closely followed by Mrs Cloonan.

"Do excuse me, Mr Brightly, won't you, Sir," she said as she moved in front of him to put the tea things down on a small wrought-iron table that matched the small chair. And then, sympathetically, "I do hope you're having a nice visit."

Brightly could see Arabella gritting her teeth as the housekeeper pottered about and prepared to pour the tea.

"That's all right, Mrs Cloonan, I'll see to that. Thank you."

"Thank you, Ma'am."

As she turned to go, Arabella called her back in a tight voice.

"Oh, Mrs Cloonan."

The housekeeper turned back by this time aware of the tension.

"Could you help me, please?" Arabella

said with forced sweetness, having just intercepted the frenetic canine nuisance with a roughness which had produced a definite winded yelp. "Mr Brightly has just told me I have a lot of debts and no money, and I seem to be in danger of murdering the dog."

Mrs Cloonan said "Oh, you poor thing!" and made clucking noises which likewise were not exclusively directed either to the dog or to its mistress but contrived to seem sympathetic to both. She swept the offending animal up to what, in less exalted literature than this, would be flatly—or perhaps not flatly—described as her ample bosom.

When she had gone, Brightly said reassuringly:

"Things aren't *entirely* black, I'm glad to say. One thing you do own outright—the *Phoenix*. Though I'm afraid she'll have to be sold to pay the debts."

"The—*Phoenix?*" Arabella was lost.

"Still tied up down in Marseille, is she?"

"Marseille? Well, I suppose . . . well, as far as I . . ." Then, giving up and shrugging helplessly: "What's the *Phoenix?*"

Brightly stared in astonishment.

"Good God, you don't mean you . . . she's your yacht, Mrs Tatenor."

"My *yacht?*"

73

"Pretty near half a million worth, thank heaven. But it's amazing—he never even told you about your own yacht?"

Arabella trailed the pink-nailed toes of one foot on the floor, propelling the wicker-work seat around in a series of meaningless little oscillating circles.

"Charles always told me everything," she said weakly and vacantly.

3

Simon Templar made an early start next morning. There was some exploring he wanted to do in the neighbourhood of the *Candecour*'s incineration now that the publicity had died down and he could hope to find the area reasonably clear of ghoulish or inquisitive sightseers.

The weather was calmer than it had been on that memorable day when he had last set out in the *Privateer* on the course he now set. He had an almost dead-flat sea.

Soon the sweeping bight of Christchurch Bay was lying to his starboard exactly as when Tatenor's boat had veered off towards the shore.

This morning the Saint had deliberately

not shaved and had left his dark hair tousled after an early-morning dip in the sea. An old tweed flat cap he had unearthed in a local junk-shop made an odd but not impossible match with the muddy dungarees and moth-eaten sweater he had conjured from elsewhere: which was exactly the appearance of amiable eccentricity which he needed for the beachcombing project he had set himself.

It was near high water when he reached the shore at Hengistbury Head. He beached the *Privateer* near the quiet western end and began his search, not confining himself to the beach itself but also poking and rooting among the dunes which backed on to it. Occasionally he stuffed something into his battered canvas hold-all to keep up appearances for the odd few holidaymakers who watched him curiously from time to time. In this way he gradually acquired a collection of soggy driftwood, bits of glass, cigarette packets and other useless detritus for later quiet dumping.

He had been wise in his decision to begin at the western end of the beach, about half a mile along from the site of the explosion. Even then, it took him a good six and a half hours of searching—in a pattern of coverage that was a lot more systematic than it might have appeared—before he found what he was looking for.

A corner of glass which lay exposed and glinting in the sun brought him to the spot near a grassy dune; and it only took him a minute or so to dig all the equipment out, after checking that he was unobserved.

There was a swim-mask, flippers, weighted belt and compact backpack-and-breathing-pipe assembly.

In short, a complete scuba outfit.

Simon had uncovered it only to satisfy himself that it was indeed what he thought it was, and was still shiny enough to have been put there quite recently. It was. He buried it again and proceeded to the second stage of his expedition.

For this his eccentric garb might not be ideal, but he thought it would do. He walked briskly along the foreshore until he came to the narrow stretch of water—a mere fifty yards or so across—which forms the entrance to Christchurch Harbour and divides Hengistbury's curled fingertip from the main coastline at Mudeford, a pleasant seaside village.

As he had done his swimming for the day, he hailed an old local salt who was reclining in a rowing-boat on the other side. A cool breeze had sprung up during the day.

"Can you take me across?" he called out amiably.

In due course an eye was opened and a pair of lips moved. But the man's reply was a jumbled confusion of palatals lost on the wind.

Then the boatman held up both fists and opened his ten fingers to indicate his price.

"Ten shillings!" the Saint muttered under his breath. "Dick Turpin at least wore a mask." But he signalled his agreement and the man inched his way across the water with rhythmically plodding oars.

"D'you do this every day?" Simon asked conversationally, when the plodding had been resumed in the opposite direction with himself aboard. "Row people back and forth, I mean."

The man spat out a well-masticated wad of tobacco into the sea. He had a leathery red face; his blue eyes were watery and deeply recessed behind inscrutable walls of eyebrow and eyelid.

"Aas roik. Meamoi maik," he said gruffly.

"Ah," said the Saint, without the foggiest notion of what the man had said, but gathering that the general sense of the answer as affirmative. "You must see a lot of people, then—different people." This, Simon was uncomfortably aware, was not destined to be remembered among his more sparkling pieces of dialogue. "I suppose that might help to keep it from getting too boring."

The boatman looked at him quizzically from under sunbleached eyebrows.

"Aaredaiz doant zee mahren wunniz dahg."

The Saint thought he might have caught an entire syllable here: he was almost sure he had heard the word "don't." He took encouragement and plunged on.

"I'm hoping to find out what happened to a friend of mine who may have gone missing down this way a few days ago," he said, articulating with special care as if in compensation. "As a matter of fact it was on the same day as the boat-race accident just down here and he was due to travel up to London that evening. But he never arrived. He had no car, so I suppose he would have been meaning to use the train. What would be the nearest station around here?"

The man manoeuvred the boat into its berth. He chewed steadily and slowly for a while on another wad of tobacco while the

78

watery eyes regarded the Saint. Then he spoke.

He said: "Oiklaff."

"You . . . what?" queried the Saint, for once helplessly stuck for something to say.

"Oiklaff," said the boatman more loudly and positively.

"Oiklaff?" the Saint repeated weakly.

"Aas roik," said the man, as if giving encouragement to a moron. "Eedaga'a trine a Lunnun frathahr ahrroik."

Simon's aural deciphering system reeled under the strain, clutched desperately at the "Lunnun", which could have been interpreted as "London", and shifted into a higher gear to begin coming to grips with the rest.

"A train!" he almost shouted in triumph after a pause. "He could have got a train from there. From *Highcliffe!*"

"Aas wah'oisaad, Oiklaff. Eecada gahnnair boi the bahs."

"Ah, there's a bus, is there?" Simon said, mainly to convince himself he had it right. "And how far's Highcliffe from here?"

The man spat out another tobacco wad.

"Bate foive moiwe."

"And do you happen to know when the next bus goes?"

The boatman fumbled for an ancient pocket watch and studied it interminably.

"Bate aafenaouer fmnay," he said at last.

"I see," said the Saint with a sense of real accomplishment. "I think you said ten bob. Here's a quid for your time. And thanks for the information."

He proceeded in due course to Highcliffe station with his investigatory aplomb more shaken than it had been in a long time. He had had some experience of the mild nasal burr of the typical Hampshireman—Vic Cullen was a good example—but nothing had quite prepared him for the primordial accent he had just encountered.

He approached the ticket clerk at the station in a distinctly wary frame of mind. The ticket clerk turned out to be a small, fastidiously moustached man of Indian or Pakistani origin. There was a conspicuous absence of other staff, and the little dark man radiated the air of being himself not only the ticket seller but also parcels porter, sweeper-up, lavoratory cleaner, and stationmaster—all of which indeed he was.

He eyed Simon shrewdly.

"Vhat can I do for you, Sir?"

"I'm looking for information. Not quite the ordinary sort, though."

He told his story of the friend who had failed to turn up in London when expected. The stationmaster's quick dark eyes never left Simon's face.

"Can you describe this—friend of yours?"

"Middle aged, stocky build, short greyish hair. Speaks with an accent."

The man nodded.

"He vas here. I remember him distinctly. This is an exceptionally quiet station for the most part, and I am far more than aweragely obserwant, though I say so myself. This man spoke vith, I should say, a French accent. Yes, I vould be practically certain that he was a Frenchman. He bought a single ticket to Vaterloo, and I saw him get on the train."

The quick dark eyes flicked over Simon's tall, somewhat untidily dressed figure, and he continued:

"You must understand ve don't see many foreign passengers through this station. Ours are mostly from Birmingham or Manchester, or they are locals. This man vas different. But he had no bags, and he didn't look like a tourist."

"You'd make a good court witness," Simon observed.

"Thank you," said the little man. "But

there's one thing more." He hesitated a moment. "I don't think this Frenchman was really your friend as you told me—Mr Templar."

"Now wait a minute—"

"No," put in the station-man quickly, holding up a restraining hand. "Please don't try to pull the vool ower my eyes any further. I have seen enough photographs of the notorious Simon Templar to be quite certain that you are indeed that adwenturous personage. Therefore it vould be quite pointless to persist in denying it or in maintaining your story of a friend who failed to turn up somevhere. You vere in the boat race. Putting together the ewidence, I vould wenture a hypothesis as follows."

The little man paused for breath, and Simon blinked in sheer disbelief as he continued with assured fluency.

"You have conjectured, have you not, that there was something decidedly fishy about the explosion in which Mr Charles Tatenor and his French co-driver vere killed—or rather, in which both of them were *apparently* killed. Further, I surmise from your present somevhat wagabond appearance, and your presence at my station, that you have perhaps already accumulated some ewidence

82

to support the hypothesis that the Frenchman escaped the explosion, having planned the entire episode beforehand, and leawing an unconscious or already dead man in the boat in his place. I suspect that you have been searching and have found something on the beach. There is sand on your shoes," he concluded simply.

Simon Templar swallowed hard.

"What is your name?" he asked weakly.

"John Matthew Thomas Bartholomew Chatterjee," said the stationmaster promptly and proudly.

"John Matthew," Simon told him, "you have restored my faith in the power of human articulation. Tonight your name will be added to my regional directory of back-up brainpower. Whenever I need a second opinion or some help with a difficult bit of inferential reasoning, I'll definitely consider calling you in."

Chatterjee smiled radiantly, exhibiting a set of dazzling white teeth.

"You are too amiable a man to have made such an utterance in any spirit of sarcasm," he declared. "Therefore I thank you. It vill be a privilege to assist such a notorious desperado should an occasion ewer present itself vhen I may be of service."

"But there's one proviso." Here the Saint leaned forward unsmiling, with a face hard as flint. "You so much as whisper a word of this to anyone—and I mean anyone—and I promise that you'll assist me in quite another way. I promise I'll make a point of using you for the practical exercises in the correspondence course I'm taking in amateur brain surgery. Do you read me?"

Chatterjee nodded vigorously, the white-toothed smile even broader than before.

"Indeed I do. Loud and clear. Your varning, Mr Templar, is admirably explicit, not to say drolly vorded. I completely see and understand your point of view. I shall, of course, be the wery soul of discretion. You may be confident that no third party vhatever shall be priwy to our secret. Should anybody chance to question me—for example a custodian of the law—I shall feign total incapacity to recall details of the passengers who pass daily under my eyes. I shall explain, vhile regretting sincerely, the long-standing inadequacy of my memory for faces . . ."

At some point Simon slipped quietly away and back to the *Privateer* by the way he had come. It was well into the evening before he reached his hotel room in Cowes, and after

84

a bath and leisurely dinner he fell readily into bed.

The astonishing little stationmaster's analysis left little to be added, as far as the Saint's present knowledge went. The evidence certainly seemed to point to Fournier's having set it all up. He could have knocked Tatenor out, kept out of sight himself while he steered the boat towards the shore, then turned the wheel and jumped clear on the blind side at the crucial moment, surfacing quietly farther along the beach and lying low till the fuss had died down. It was feasible—even if it did mean that Fournier was a lot cleverer than Simon had been inclined to give him credit for.

Of course, there was still the second body to be explained. Complete with crash helmet. But the *Candecour* was one of the few boats in the race big enough to hide a body, either an unconscious body or one that was already a corpse . . . The Candecorpse . . . The Saint's thoughts veered and his eyelids drooped as he drifted back and forth across the hazy margins of sleep and waking. Fournier must have smuggled the body aboard after the scrutineer's main inspection on the eve of the race. Odd name, *Candecour*. He'd been pondering on it. And on Tatenor. That was an odd name too. What did it mean, anyway? And Tatenor spoke perfect, but pairrfect, French. Monsieur Teteneur . . . or how about *Tête noire?* Monsieur Blackhead. Like the French used to call the Algerian colonists *pieds noirs*. Mr Blackhead is dead . . . something shady about him—a bit of a black sheep . . . sheep . . . sleep.

The Saint slept.

—4—

On that same evening, less than two hours before, Arabella Tatenor, breaking her journey to Marseilles, had parked her red MG tourer in front of a country hotel near Orleans and booked in for the night.

Her decision to zoom south-of-France-wards post-haste had been made the instant the solicitor's gloomy and mostly unwelcome news had finally sunk in. Which was about forty-five seconds after he had stopped apologising, prised his rear end up out of the torturous garden chair, and said his goodbyes.

"Now, Mrs Cloonan, don't fuss!" she had remonstrated good-humouredly in response to the housekeeper's mild demurrer. "It's not the North Pole or the lower regions of hell—it's just France."

"Well, exactly," Mrs Cloonan had said dubiously. "France." The syllable might have been synonymous with "sin" as she pronounced it. "You driving by yourself in France is what I'm thinking of—with all those fifty million Frenchmen there, or whatever it is, and on the wrong side of the road, too!"

Arabella had smiled at that. She knew that Mrs Cloonan was genuinely fond of her and concerned for her well-being.

"They're not all like Fournier, thank goodness!" she told her soothingly. "And I've driven in France before, you know. Actually you get used to it very quickly. And the French countryside's marvellous, and the road to Marseilles is hardly a foot-path." Arabella grinned. "So stop worrying. I promise I'll call you, the first overnight stop I make."

That was Arabella Tatenor. She had to go to Marseille? Very well, then go she would. Right away. Or as near right away as could comfortably be managed.

She had seen the MG and herself safely aboard the eight o'clock ferry to Southampton on the morning after Brightly's visit. From Southampton—which in those days had no direct ferry link with France—she had driven the seventy-five miles along the south coast to Newhaven in good time to catch the one o'clock boat to Dieppe; and some five hours later she had driven the MG off the boat and on to a French quay. The French customs formalities had delayed her only a minute or so, mostly taken up with a stylish piece of ogling from a raffish-looking *douanier* who wielded the chalk of his species, with, Arabella thought, unusual panache.

And then she had emerged into the sun-shine of a late Normandy afternoon, and within minutes she was zipping through that rich green countryside, so hauntingly like yet unlike its English counterpart a mere hundred miles back across the water. She had driven contentedly for the better part of four hours—and not so contentedly for the worse part.

The worse part was driving through the towns that straddle the main road—towns like Rouen and Evreux, Dreux and Chartres—every one of which meant a two- or three-kilometre intrusion of those cobbles so beloved of the French and so bone-jarring to anyone travelling in a firmly sprung sports car.

Daylight was dissolving into the transparency of a star-spangled night when she pulled up outside the hotel, a few miles beyond Orleans. The place looked as if it had once been a barn; all half-timbered and skew-whiff, it had a warm, friendly look and an obviously active restaurant. And it had the name *Hôtel des Anglais*, which at least offered prospect of sympathetic welcome for weak speakers of French, in which category Arabella unreservedly placed herself.

She chose the hotel for these reasons and because it happened to come into view at the right moment. But the two occupants of the ordinary black Citroen that pulled up outside the same hotel a minute or so later, after she had gone inside with her suitcase, chose it for a very different reason.

They chose it because they had followed her, very carefully and discreetly, all the way from Cowes, and they had not the slightest intention of losing her now.

She had settled herself in the hotel's restaurant and was preparing to order her dinner when the fat man came in and sat down at a neighbouring table.

The fatness made the sitting down into a rather protracted operation. Arabella watched the performance discreetly but with more than normal curiosity. She had a vague feeling that there was something familiar about the fat man; but it was no more than that, and for the moment she dismissed it.

He was large generally, but his midriff was of a vast and pendulous corpulence out of proportion to the rest of him. Arabella noticed with concealed amusement that he had to sit well back from the table to leave room for that great wobbling paunch. His sparse greying hair was matched by a similarly greying but luxuriant moustache that drooped to give him the look of an ageing Mexican *bandido*.

The impression, however, was contradicted by his clothing, which was so incongruously dapper that Arabella had to control herself sternly to keep from giggling out loud. His trousers were immaculate light-grey flannels, belted at the waist—which in his case meant somewhere on the re-entrant undersurface of that ballooning midriff. At least two of his chins were camouflaged by a startlingly debonair cravat, and the upper part of his pear-shaped torso was gift-wrapped absurdly in the type of blazer in which lean young men at Cambridge once used to look dashing.

Arabella's attention dwelt only briefly on these details of the fat man. She was too hungry to trouble herself about where, if anywhere, she might have seen him before, or someone who resembled him. She was impatient to catch the eye of the white-jacketed waiter, an apparently world-weary old retainer of a type still found in some French provincial hotels. He had a face like a cross between a pensioned-off clown and a tired bloodhound, and he seemed quietly determined, in the traditional manner of waiters, that his eye should not be caught. He pottered busily at a corner trolley with napkins and cutlery, or straightened a table-cloth here and there, giving the impression that such engrossing exertions could easily fill his entire day.

Arabella toyed with the menu impatiently. She was about to call out when the fat man beat her to it.

"Monsieur!"

The voice was a rich bass, full of author-ity. He rapped imperiously on the table, snapped his fingers and assumed an expres-sion of fierce chivalry, as the startled waiter came towards him.

"The young lady is waiting to be served," he told him in French. *"S'il vous plaît!"*

"Mais certainement." The waiter turned to Arabella. "I am sorry you have been kept waiting."

"De rien," Arabella said after nodding her thanks to the fat man. And she continued in rather hesitant French. "I should like to have, first, some hors d'oeuvres, and afterwards the *filet mignon,* medium, with a green salad."

The fat man watched with his head cocked slightly on one side.

"Permit me to advise you, Madame," he put in, in English. "I could not avoid to overhear your order. May I suggest, if you are considering a wine, the *Château Durfort-Vivens?* It is a fine Bordeaux wine, most reasonably priced." The fat man hesitated. "Indeed, if you will permit a further liberty, I too will be feasting on *le filet mignon de Charolais* and I will be honoured if you will join me at the table and share with me a bottle of the *Château Durfort-Vivens.*"

"Well, I don't know . . ." Arabella looked appraisingly at the fat man. He was what Mrs Cloonan would undoubtedly have called "rather forward", but he might well make an interesting dinner companion. She wavered. The baggy-featured waiter glanced from one to the other.

Arabella made up her mind.

"Why, yes, I should like that. Thank you."

The fat man beamed. After he had dispatched the waiter with a barrage of instructions, Arabella sat down at his table.

"Well, well," he said, as he un-Gallically tucked one corner of a napkin behind his cravat—making himself look like a vast nursery Tweedledum—"a remarkable coincidence, is it not, Madame Tatenor?"

Arabella stared at him startled.

"I beg your pardon. Do I know you?"

The fat Frenchman spread his hands apologetically.

"In truth, it is I who should beg yours. Perhaps I should have pretended not to recognise you, rather than place myself in the necessity for reminding you of what must be most distressing. Perhaps you did not notice? Quite understandable in the circumstances. You see, I was in the courtroom during the inquest on your unfortunate husband. It was a terrible tragedy, but terrible. And you are a widow so young." He shrugged to convey the hopelessness of trying to put these things into words. "You have my deepest sympathies."

"Thank you. Now that you mention it, I think I do recall seeing you in court."

The fat man allowed himself a restrained smile, and twirled his moustache with magnificent resignation.

"Madame—I am difficult to overlook altogether." He patted his gross midriff affectionately. "A consequence, I am afraid, of gastronomic excess. A lifelong habit which I am now too old, fortunately, to consider breaking . . . But what am I thinking of? I am shamefully forgetting the manners. I must introduce myself. I am Jacques Descartes. I was making on the island some negotiations in a matter of bulls and cows. Now I am returning to my home in the south, I drive with my assistant until we tire, then we stop at this delightful hotel and—suddenly, there in the restaurant, *quelle surprise!* Whom do I see but the beautiful—you permit me, Madame?—the beautiful Madame Tatenor. It is a little world, is it not? Such a little world!"

"It certainly is," Arabella agreed. And then for conversation's sake she added: "Whereabouts in the south is your home? I suppose you're some kind of—farmer?"

Descartes winced at the word.

"Not a farmer, Madame. No, no! I am an *entrepreneur* of the bullfighting in France. I am a breeder and trainer of the picador horses, also a breeder of bulls. You know, perhaps, that not only the Spanish have their bulls and picadors. I have my *haras* in the village of St Martin-du-Marais, in the Camargue. There I live, and there I own also an hotel. It is true I have also several local farms under my wings, but that is purely a business operation. My horses and bulls, they are my real love. My associates and I are proud, most proud, of our successes."

"And—if I may ask without seeming too nosey—was your trip to England, to the island, a success, would you say?"

Descartes hesitated.

"Let me put it in this way. I have a . . . a lead to follow up, which could prove to be most rewarding. Most rewarding. Oh yes, I think you can say that our trip was well worth while."

"But what happened to the assistant you mentioned?" Arabella enquired. "Isn't he hungry?"

Descartes smiled broadly, exhibiting some expensive gold dental work.

"Enrico is indisposed. He is not at all a good traveller when a passenger, I am afraid. So he sleeps now. And it is good. Tomorrow he will drive, and when driving he will not feel sick. It is so with some people."

"How about you? Will you feel queasy when *he's* driving?"

"Definitely not. My digestive system has become hardened during all the years of abuse—glorious abuse!" Descartes leaned forward, as far as his midriff would allow, with a confiding and avuncular manner. "I confess, Madame Tatenor, I am an incorrigible gourmand. Food is for me a grand passion, perhaps the grand passion I failed to find with a woman. But life is so, *n'est-ce-pas?* We find our compensations. For example, I detect, do I not, the arrival of our *hors d'oeuvres!*"

They continued to chat amiably over the food, and Arabella found that time passed pleasantly enough in Descartes' ebullient company.

"You're something of a philosopher yourself, aren't you?" she observed an hour and a half later, over the *cognac*. "Like your famous namesake."

He beamed.

"You are right. I too, in my way, am a

thinker. Perhaps not quite in the class of the great René Descartes . . . but then, there is one enterprise of logical thinking in which even he might not be the match of me. I say so, Madame, with all modesty. That enterprise is—do you by chance play the game of backgammon?"

"Backgammon?" Arabella cast back through her memory. "Why yes, I do believe I played that a few times in my college days. What's it called in French?"

"It is called *le tric-trac*. And I—" Descartes puffed out his chest proudly, but the expansion of his midriff was manifestly greater and Arabella's composure teetered on the brink for a difficult moment "—in certain circles I am known as *Jacques du tric-trac*. I am, with modesty, probably the finest backgammon player in all France."

Arabella raised a polite but ironic eyebrow.

"Only in France?"

"Possibly even in the entire world. Although there is Schneider, and I suppose there is Guggisheimer."

"Guggisheimer?"

"An American player of some reputation. Doubtless he has a certain talent." Descartes shrugged in a manner dismissive of

Guggisheimer. "One day I shall test this talent of his for myself."

Arabella cupped her hands under the brandy glass and swirled the amber liquid around appreciatively.

"Come to think of it, Charles—my husband—once told me he used to play backgammon a lot. I mean competitively."

"Oh yes, your husband was a player . . . ?" The question mark was applied so lightly, almost as an afterthought, that Arabella looked sharply at Descartes.

"You didn't—you didn't know my husband?"

Descartes hesitated for a moment, then shook his head. "An Englishman called Charles Tatenor? No, Madame, I never knew him. But tell me about him, if it is not too painful. What kind of a man was he?"

"Charles?" Arabella mused for a while. "Oh, I guess he was as English as they come. The quintessential uppercrust sporting Englishman. Plummy accent, vague profession; something or other in property that paid the bills and let him indulge his taste for expensive sports, like powerboat racing, horses, gambling, and women. In short, all the vices of the upper set."

Descartes smiled another smile in which peripheral dental gold gleamed under the canopy of the bandit moustache.

"You are very frank and direct, Madame. I enjoy the conversation to be so. But the typical Englishman—he has not only the vices, I trust? Or sometimes the vices are also the virtues or the attractions, is it not so?"

"That's true. But there was one thing about Charles that was very untypical of the English. He was exceptionally good at languages. You know how the English have this reputation, like the Americans, they don't usually bother much with foreign languages, and when they do, well, the accent's atrocious. But Charles spoke French and German fantastically well. To my ear, perfectly. Though he was strangely modest about it, almost secretive actually. But just occasionally the need would arise, and I was always amazed at his fluency. There's no doubt he was a very clever man."

Descartes, who had been listening attentively, nodded vigorously.

"Certainly, Mr Tatenor was extremely clever—from what you say, Madame . . . But allow me to be direct in revealing my curiosity. May I ask what brings you to

France, so to speak pell mell upon your husband's most regrettable death?"

Arabella was at her ease with the fat Frenchman by this juncture and saw nothing untoward in the question. Yet some instinct, which was more than simple reticence over her financial status, but which she couldn't have analysed at the time, made her keep back a part of the story.

"I'm going to Marseilles to admire a yacht," she told him.

Descartes looked puzzled.

"A yacht?"

"Charles had had this yacht for years, apparently, but he never said a word about it to me. And now she's mine. So I'm going down there to look her over for myself."

Descartes nodded slowly and thoughtfully, and the gold dental work flashed briefly again.

"That is completely understandable," he said. "In your place, I too would speed at once in the direction of such a property. It is exciting, I am sure, to find oneself suddenly the owner of a substantial possession which one has never yet seen."

"Exactly."

"Then you are driving on to Marseille tomorrow?" It was more a statement than a question. "But what a fortunate coincidence!" he added softly. "My village is directly on your route, only an hour or so before Marseille. I will insist, Madame, that you will accept the hospitality of my hotel for tomorrow night."

III: How the Saint missed the Boat, and Arabella came down to Earth.

——1——————————

Morning brought Simon Templar a large manilla envelope, which he soon had cause to wish had been in his possession a day sooner.

It was from Beaky. The Saint opened it and took out three photographs and two typewritten sheets of paper. He glanced at the photographs briefly, then put them aside. He picked up the typewritten sheets and read.

Photographs you sent of man on boat are of Maurice Tranchier (France). Born Lyons, age 43. Three convictions France for armed robbery, latest 11 years ago for international bullion robbery when French launch carrying 20 million francs in gold bars was seized en route to Morocco from Marseille.

Tranchier released three years ago after serving 8 years of a 10-year sentence; likewise three accomplices in same crime:

Jacques Descartes (France), Enrico Bernadotti (Italy), Pancho Gomez (Spain).

Fourth accomplice and probable ring-
leader believed to be Karl Schwarzkopf
(Switzerland). Escaped with launch and
gold. Schwarzkopf remains untraced; gold
remains unrecovered. Suspected fifth accomplice, on Algerian side, also never
traced.
Descartes, Bernadotti and Gomez known
to be living in village of St Martin-du-
Marais in Camargue region of S. France.
Descartes regarded as most dangerous.
Owns several properties, hotel and stud
farm; believed to practise local
intimidation/protection. French police so
far unable to obtain adequate evidence.

Karl Schwarzkopf: Born Bern, age (if living) 48. Graduated Geneva at 22 with
highest linguist honours. Native language
Swiss German dialect; known to be completely fluent in High German, French
and English. No criminal record. Was
employee of international bank involved
in bullion transfer; based Paris, 6 years,
vanished at time of robbery.

The Saint picked up the three photographs. One had the name *Jacques Descartes* on the back; it was of the fat man he had seen in the courtroom. Another was of the swarthy, lizard-like man who had been with him; and it was marked *Enrico Bernadotti*. And the third photograph was of *Pancho Gomez;* it showed a sullen thick-lipped face with tiny piggy eyes buried deep beneath the overhanging brow of a markedly asymmetrical head. The Saint had never seen Señor Gomez before; nor did the photograph make him long for Señor Gomez's acquaintance.

The absence of a photograph of the missing man was of no real significance. The Saint needed no photograph; the name was enough. It sprang out at him from the typewritten sheet: Karl Schwarzkopf. The surname, not uncommon in German, translated directly into English made only the ridiculous "Blackhead", with its inescapable associations with acne. But in French it came out as *"Tête noire"*. And it took no great effort of imagination, once you had got that far, to see "Tatenor" as an English derivative of that French translation of the German original . . . Tatenor the man was certainly linguistic sophisticate enough to have arrived at Tatenor, the name, by that circuitous trilingual route.

So much of the story fitted that Simon had no doubt at all in his mind. Tatenor was—or had been—the missing man Schwarzkopf. As soon as the trick with the names had come clear, some of Simon's other rambling half-awake thoughts of the night before fell likewise into place, and he saw that a similar piece of linguistic juggling could plausibly explain the name of Tatenor's boat. If you started with the German for speedboat (or race-boat), which was *Rennboot*, and translated that literally into French, you got *canot de course*; and from there it was an easy step to probably the simplest abbreviation, *Candecour*.

So Schwarzkopf the Swiss had vanished after the bullion robbery, leaving his accomplices to take the rap while he took the gold. And then Schwarzkopf the Swiss had become Tatenor the Englishman—if anything, a more English Englishman than most of the native-born kind. That he had been able to pull it off was a remarkable testimony to his linguistic talent—added to the national advantage the Swiss have in that respect.

And then, eleven years later, one of those

accomplices—Tranchier, calling himself Fournier—had caught up with him. And it took little imagination to guess that he had come for his—or their collective—share of the loot.

And on the evidence the Saint had discovered, it looked as if he might have got what he had come for. And yet—why were the others here? Had Tranchier now run out on *them?* One thing was certain: if the loot was still in the form of gold bars, Tranchier was not carrying it with him.

Simon tried to put himself in Schwarzkopf's place after the robbery. He would almost certainly have aimed to keep the gold and convert it into cash gradually, rather than raise suspicions by trying to sell off that quantity all at once. He would have reckoned to "spend" the gold over a period of years. And he would have needed a safe place to stash it away, gold being far too heavy to lug about. So, Schwarzkopf would most likely have hidden the gold somewhere and returned at intervals to draw from his private "bank". The odds were, then, that Tranchier, before he had killed Schwarzkopf, had extracted from him the necessary information and means of access to the remaining gold.

But again Simon came back to the other two he had seen. What did they want? Not Tranchier, presumably. They had no reason not to accept his death as fact—as far as the Saint knew. Therefore they must be there to continue what, as far as their knowledge could be presumed to go, Tranchier had failed to accomplish . . .

And then it came to Simon with the blinding clarity of the newly obvious. There was only one person left from whom they might expect to discover where that gold was.

That person was his widow.

Arabella.

Already uneasy, the Saint was climbing into the silver Aston Martin almost before he drew that final inference.

He drove straight to Arabella's house.

At the back of his mind ever since the court hearing had been that nagging discomfort he had still not managed to explain to himself, the first seeds of which had been sown when he had seen the two men he now knew as Descartes and Bernadotti. As he now saw, his reaction to them had amounted to an instinctive awareness that their interest in Tatenor's death was somehow more than casual. Now, Simon cursed himself for not listening much earlier, and with closer attention, to that inner voice of disquiet; and it was with a definite foreboding of trouble ahead that he drove up the crunching gravel approach to the house.

Mrs Cloonan was pottering about in the front garden.

"Why, bless me, sir, if you haven't missed her by a day," she told him. "She's gone to France. The south of France. Marseilles." She pronounced it *"Mah-sales"*.

Simon was not altogether surprised to find her gone. Arabella was an independent-minded woman and there was no reason she shouldn't shoot off to France if the fancy took her. But he was curious, nevertheless, about the rather abrupt manner of her departure—especially as they had had at least a half-arrangement to meet within a day or two.

"The South of France," he repeated, with raised eyebrows. "Rather a spur-of-the-moment young widow, isn't she? Did she take her black bikini?"

Mrs Cloonan did her best to look shocked.

"Oh, sir! I do declare, I never heard such a thing!" She clucked reprovingly, but with a twinkle in her eye. "But truth be told, well . . ." She looked around conspiratorially, satisfied herself that the nearby bushes contained no obvious eavesdroppers and continued almost in a whisper: ". . .what with Mr Tatenor passing away as he did, and all—I gather she had to go down to try and sell her yacht, sir."

"Her yacht," murmured the Saint. "Poor thing."

"Yes, sir. But she does seem in better spirits. She phoned me from France last night. She was staying in a nice little hotel, she said, near Orleans. Playing backgammon, she said—with some great blimp of a Frenchman."

For an instant the Saint's heart stopped; and then a ghostly millipede with icicles for feet scuttled up his spine. It was thanks only to an automatic self-control, bred in him over long years of practice, that neither of these two events produced more than the merest ripple on the outer surface of his casual demeanour.

"A fat Frenchman who likes to play backgammon? Well, he sounds harmless enough to the ladies, as Frenchmen go," he quipped.

Mrs Cloonan beamed.

"Exactly what I thought myself, sir. And she said he'd been most civil, and entertaining, and helpful. Oh, and tonight, she's going to be staying at his hotel, in the

South . . . Why, is something wrong, Mr Templar?"

Even the Saint's aforementioned self-control must have let him down fractionally when he heard that final piece of news. He hastily assured Mrs Cloonan that there was nothing to worry about, and then took his leave of her.

He had been, he knew, careless. He could have thought of at least a dozen past occasions in his life when a like degree of carelessness would have cost him that life. And his life was a possession he did not regard lightly.

"Simon Templar, old son," he told himself sternly as he drove back to the hotel, "you're getting careless."

He certainly couldn't excuse himself for failing to foresee at least the possibility of developments involving Arabella, nor for playing his cards so close to the chest and giving her the impression that he regarded the whole affair as closed.

There was only one practical course of action open to him now; and that was to pack a few things of his own and set off after her.

He was a whole day behind, but the likelihood was that Arabella would be safe at least until she checked into Descartes' hotel in the south that evening. That "come into my parlour" establishment had to be the Saint's immediate and direct destination.

Ten minutes on the telephone to travel agents was enough to establish that there was no available combination of air and surface transport that would get him to the village of St Martin-du-Marais in under eighteen hours. He knew he should be able to do it by car and ferry in several hours less than that.

Minutes later he was skimming across the water in the *Privateer* towards Vic Cullen's boatyard at Bursledon, on Southampton Water, where he had left the Hirondel; and within another half hour he was weaving the big red-and-cream car skillfully and at a highly illegal speed along the south coast road towards Newhaven. It was almost eleven, and the ferry was due to leave at one. Drivers had to be at the quay half an hour beforehand. Simon reckoned that he might still get on if he arrived as late as 12.45, but that still gave him only an hour and three quarters to travel those seventy-five miles, in far from open-road conditions.

First the outskirts of Portsmouth loomed up, with an infuriating succession of dawdling drivers in wood-trimmed Morris Minors; then Havant and Chichester, then Worthing and Brighton. He drove with tremendous verve and skill, with the needle nudging up beyond sixty on every brief occasion when a burst of speed was possible. But there was a limit to what even the Saint and the Hirondel together could do in the thick and almost constant traffic, and he arrived at the Newhaven quay at three minutes to one, just as the ferry, its loading completed, was preparing to leave.

There was nothing he could do but sit and watch helplessly as it slowly backed out of its berth, announcing its departure with a single prolonged trump of what sounded, in the circumstances, very much like derision.

—2—

After another rapid investigation of options, the Saint had to conclude that there was nothing else for it but to wait there for the next boat—four hours later.

It was after 9 o'clock that night when he finally drove the Hirondel off the boat at Dieppe and started on the long haul south. Not for the first time, he was glad that he still had the Hirondel to rely on, after the years of service it had given him. Now, with long distances to cover at speed on fairly open and deserted roads, the car would come into its own with a vengeance. The great flamboyant vehicle thrived on a challenge, and it was for the sake of times like these, remembered and anticipated, that Simon Templar had kept it, year after year, despite the blandishments and the sometimes real temptations offered by newer and discreeter vehicles.

There never had been a car quite like the Hirondel, and there never would be again. That magnificent monster, that opulent and now splendidly dated conveyance that drew every eye back for a second ogle—and a third—went, if possible, even better than its looks promised. From the low-throated throb of its eight cylinders to the deep muted rasp of its near-racing exhaust, it promised, and delivered, the exhilaration of sheer power. Unstoppably, tirelessly, it carved its way through the air, its huge-tyred wheels thrusting mile after mile of road and countryside behind it. The Saint met little traffic on that five-hundred-and-fifty-mile drive south, and he covered the distance in an astonishing eleven hours, including a couple of essential stops. For most of the distance the Hirondel's powerful headlamps sliced a bright wedge through the Gallic dark; for the last hundred miles or so the sky lightened through a grey-and-pink dawn.

It was just about eight o'clock when he pulled up in the Camargue village of St Martin-du-Marais. The hotel was easy enough to find, being slap in the middle of what was anyway a small village. It was a compact hotel and had doubtless once been unimposing; now, its exterior had some of the incongruous flamboyance of its owner himself, an effect achieved mostly by the use of large, elaborately curlicued, multicolored lettering for the name: *Hôtel Descartes*.

Simon opened the front door and went in. The cramped lobby smelt of the morning's coffee and croissants, and a hint of last night's *bourguignonne* still hung on the air, along with the fumes from a cigarette the *concierge* was smoking.

The *concierge*, a small weedy cynical-looking man in rolled-up shirtsleeves, looked as though he had been on duty all night and had stayed awake some of the time. When Simon opened the door from the street, he was standing by the reception counter scanning the morning paper. A cleaning cloth and water bucket were by his feet.

"I'm looking for Madame Tatenor," Simon said in French.

The *concierge* looked up.

"Madame Tatenor?" he said. "She is departed. Perhaps one hour since."

Simon started counting to ten, and got as far as five.

"Any idea where she's heading?"

The weedy *concierge* shook his head, tapped an inch off his *Gauloise,* and shrugged.

"Marseille—maybe. I do not know."

"What about the proprietor, Monsieur Descartes?" Simon persisted. "I believe she is a friend of his—a guest. Would he perhaps know where—"

"M Descartes is not here," the man cut in. "I cannot help you any further." His manner had changed from the merely offhand to the definitely truculent. "And now, I have work to do, Monsieur."

He stubbed out the remains of the *Gauloise,* picked up the bucket and cleaning cloth, and shuffled off through one of the doorways leading from the lobby. Simon turned to go, his mouth set in a grim line.

But then unexpectedly a hoarse voice, like a stage whisper, reached him.

"Monsieur!"

He turned in the direction of the sound. It came from somewhere in the short main corridor from the lobby, from a doorway that was now being held fractionally ajar.

The Saint covered the distance to the doorway in two noiseless seconds. The door was opened wider, and he saw a young woman who might well, in normal circumstances, have been pretty. But it appeared that circumstances for her had recently been far from normal, and she was a far from pretty sight. Her face was a mass of welts and bruises; both her eyes were blackened, and her lips were cut and swollen. She was wearing a nightdress which, though by no means in the negligée class, exposed enough of her neck and shoulders to reveal bruising there too. She spoke with difficulty.

"You . . . you look for the English woman?"

Simon nodded.

"Madame Tatenor, yes. She is a friend of mine." Simon kept his own voice to a whisper and motioned his wish to join her inside the room.

116

She let him in and closed the door quietly behind them.

"I am Geneviève. Chambermaid in the hotel. I think, Monsieur," she croaked painfully, "you will not find her on the road to Marseille."

Simon spent approximately the next two and a half seconds digesting the information.

"Is she still here?" he asked.

Genevieve shook her head.

"No, Monsieur . . . she left perhaps half an hour ago."

"Alone?"

Genevieve nodded.

"In her own car?"

"Yes . . . but they have done something to her car. This morning, before it was fully light. I heard a sound, and from the window I saw him, the lizard one, Bernadotti." She made a mime of spitting in disgust, and Simon's lips came together in a hard line.

"The lizard one—Bernadotti. Did he do this to you?"

She nodded.

"I found him last night, searching Madame Tatenor's room, while she was having dinner."

The Saint said to himself, with feeling:

117

"That's one I owe you for her, Enrico old chum." For the moment he preferred not to speculate how many he might owe Enrico for Arabella by the time he caught up with her.

"Where do you think they'll have taken her?" he asked tersely.

Genevieve rummaged in a drawer.

"I will draw a plan for you so that you can look for her where you are most likely to find her," she said in that painful whispering croak. "At the *haras* of Monsieur Descartes." She paused and looked at Simon appraisingly. "I think you are a good man. Please remember, worse will happen to me if it is know that I assisted you against *them*."

"I understand," Simon told her. "I shall say nothing."

"They are very bad men." She gave a shudder. "And no one in the village would help you to find the way quickly if they thought you were no friend of these men. They have fear of these three. We all have fear of them . . . the *sadique*, the deaf one with the knife always, and that great fat *cochon*. For two years or more they have lived here. They loan money to the farmers,

118

rent to us the equipment. Now we do not exist except as *they* wish."

She had found a pencil and a piece of paper which she spread on the table with trembling fingers.

"Monsieur—you will have to be very careful. And do not hope too much. I think they will want something from her. If once they have it, they will kill her."

—3

Arabella had risen early and left the hotel at seven because she was chafing to get to Marseille and see the *Phoenix—her* yacht. Three nights had passed since she had first learnt of the *Phoenix*'s existence, and by this time her curiosity was definitely getting the better of her normal preference for late rising. Add to that the fact that the hotel itself was a reminder of two evenings spent in Descartes' ultimately wearing company, and she had a strong double reason for wanting to get on her way.

But she had got no further than a kilometre or so when the MG began behaving like a bucking bronco. Its engine seemed to have been visited by a malady of galloping indecision; it changed its mind ten or twelve times, in the space of less than a minute, about whether it wanted to run or not. Arabella pulled off the road, put the gearstick in neutral and revved the engine a few times, whereupon it made up its mind. It did not want to run. It stopped, and would not start again.

Arabella knew nothing about the tinkering her car had suffered earlier that morning at the hands of Enrico Bernadotti; she only knew that the car had broken down.

She had left the village well behind her. Traffic was virtually nonexistent—she recalled one car passing her, in the opposite direction—and there was no telephone in sight. She started walking towards a house a couple of hundred yards away, but had only covered a quarter of the distance when she heard a truck coming.

Not being one to do things by halves, she ran into the road and waved her arms excitedly in a way that left her predicament in no doubt.

The effort, as it turned out, was unnecessary. It was a breakdown truck—complete with winch. It stopped some way in front of the MG and then backed up close. Out of it jumped a short muscular blob of a man in mechanic's overalls and a cap. He was munching a sandwich, which she took to be the reason for his failure to offer a cordial greeting, or indeed any greeting at all.

Arabella's French, while it might be just about up to the simpler transactions of life, was completely unequal to the task of describing the salient details of a mechanical breakdown. She resorted to sign language and a single, far from French, word.

"Kaputt!"

She operated the starter a few times to demonstrate the car's recalcitrance. The mechanic said nothing; he simply attached the grappling-chains of his winch to the underside of her car and wound it up on to the back of the truck with Arabella still in the driver's seat. Then the truck, painted with the name *Garage Soustelle Frères*, turned around and headed back towards the village.

It went straight past the garage of that name, which she had noticed earlier, and left the village by the opposite route. After a moment's unease, Arabella settled down to wait, supposing that there must be other premises belonging to the Soustelles. But when the breakdown truck pulled right off the main road, and began following a rough dirt-track across mixed pasture land and marshy, boggy ground, she became definitely and substantively uneasy.

She leant on the horn. Nothing happened. She switched on the ignition and leant on it again. The penetrating *paa-aa-aarp* punctuated the calm of the countryside but produced no apparent effect on the breakdown driver. He continued to transport her, and her car, farther off the beaten track: through a farm gateway, along a still-rougher and less-beaten track than before; then between some trees to a stony yard between farm buildings.

The truck stopped and the driver got out, wiping the remains of his meal from his blubbery lips with the back of an oily hand.

"What the hell is this place?" Arabella began angrily. "Why have you brought me here?" She looked around at the timber fences, gates, corrals, horses; and back at the still-silent driver.

He had taken off his cap, and now his lips parted in something like a sadistic smile, revealing unpleasant-looking yellow teeth to go with his unpleasant-looking putty-nose and squinting piggy-eyes. Arabella regarded him disgustedly.

"My, but aren't you an ugly one!" she

declared, hoping to provoke some response. But he only beckoned her to follow as he set off for one of the adobe farm buildings.

He opened the door and stood aside for her to enter; then he followed her inside, shut the door, and stood firmly against it.

Arabella looked around. She was in a large farm office, well furnished in an old-fashioned heavy style, the walls liberally decorated with bullfight posters and photographs of horses—hefty brutes, many of them accoutred and padded for the bullring, some with picadors astride. At the far end was another closed door. Between Arabella and that other door, at a huge rolltop desk, sat a big man in a sombrero, with his back to her. Nearby sprawled a sallow-skinned man dressed all in black, who was picking at the strings of a guitar. His features were lizard-like, his shirt open halfway to the waist, revealing a black doormat of a torso decorated with a heavy gold chain.

The man with the guitar struck a sudden sharp chord, and the large figure at the desk swivelled to face Arabella.

Under the broad sombrero, that luxuriant bandit moustache and the huge bulk of chins beneath were unmistakable. It was Descartes.

123

"Bonjour, Madame Tatenor," he said softly. "You see, I could not bear the parting from you!"

He smiled expansively, but now, in these new surroundings, there was something menacing in that gold-fringed smile. Arabella struggled to grasp the situation.

"But what . . . what are *you* doing here?" she finally said. "I mean, what am *I* doing here?"

The black-clad lizard had put down his guitar, and now he came forward, hissing through wolfish white teeth, to favour Arabella with a close inspection.

"And who the hell are you!" she snapped without ceremony, disliking him on the instant, whoever he might be.

Descartes chuckled.

"Let me introduce my associates . . . Enrico Bernadotti, who arranged your little mechanical trouble. And your guide here,"—he inclined his head towards the blubbery-lipped man who had driven the truck—"Pancho Gomez. You may have observed, his conversational powers are limited. He is a deaf-mute."

She glanced around as Descartes' words registered.

"Arranged my breakdown? You seem to

124

have been to a lot of trouble to get me here. What do you want?"

Descartes shifted his bulk in the chair, causing the huge convexity of his midriff to wobble noticeably.

"The answer to that, Madame Tatenor," he said very sternly and seriously, "is simple." Then more silkily: "I think you know already what we want." And then his voice cracked through the air with whiplash force: "So let us get down to business!"

"What business?" she said calmly. "I really don't know what you're talking about."

She might be putting a brave front on it; but the fact was that underneath the moderately composed exterior was an interior that was not only indignant but more than a little scared. This was certainly the first time in her life that anything of the kind had happened to her, and she didn't at all like the way things were shaping up.

Descartes sighed impatiently.

"Madame Tatenor, please let us not play games. You are the widow of Charles Tatenor. The widow of our ex-partner in crime. Only that we knew him under another name."

"Crime? Another name? What *is* all this? Are you people *crazy?*"

125

Descartes suddenly propelled himself towards her at speed on his castored chair.

"We want to know *where is the gold!*" he boomed, his large face reddening with anger. "*Now* does the little bell ring?"

"No, it doesn't," Arabella said firmly. "And now, I think I'd like to go home."

Unexpectedly, his motion lithe and sudden as a cat's, Bernadotti sprang forward and slapped her resoundingly across the face—sending her sprawling back, only to be caught by the lurking Gomez and shoved forward again.

"I think we should start all over again, Mrs widow-honey," Bernadotti hissed in an oily Italian-American accent. "You gotta understand, we don't mess around."

Arabella was furious, almost murderous, but temporarily numbed into silence by the ferocity and suddenness of the blow from Bernadotti.

"Where is the money?" Descartes demanded.

"What money? What gold? Please . . . I don't know. I don't know about any money."

"Our other associate, Monsieur Fournier as he was known, did finally locate our old partner Karl . . . your husband, Mrs

126

Tatenor. But he died before he was able to tell us where to find the money, or the gold, if it remains as gold. If indeed he ever did extract the secret from your husband before he died . . . before they both died. We cannot now discover from Karl, from your Charles, where he secreted our mutual ill-gotten gains. Therefore, we must discover it from you." Descartes paused and waggled a solemn forefinger at Arabella. "Be assured, you will tell us before a long time has passed. You might save yourself pain by telling us now." He emphasised his final words with that plump stabbing forefinger: *"Where—is—the—gold?"*

She repeated herself firmly, but with an edge of desperation now: "I tell you I don't know about any gold, or money. My problem is, Charles didn't leave me any—only debts. That's why I've come here—to France, to Marseille. I've got to sell this yacht—*my* yacht, the *Phoenix* . . ."

Descartes put his head on one side and studied her for a few moments. Arabella tried again.

"I don't have any money. No money. No gold. *Comprenez-vous?"*

Descartes shook his head sadly.

"Then you are no use to us. Your memory is too bad."

"Listen, lady," Bernadotti hissed suddenly, "we know the gold or the money is here in France, where your husband once did business. All you have to do is tell us *where*."

"What money? What gold? I don't know about any money or gold!" Arabella was near snapping-point now.

Again Descartes looked at her aslant for a moment.

"Let me remind you of the facts," he began, "since you have such a poor memory, it appears. Four of us endured eight years in prison for a robbery of gold bullion in which your 'Charles' also took a part— and from which *he* escaped with the gold, all of the gold, while *we* were caught. Now we want that gold, or whatever remains of it."

"All this is news to me. If Charles had any gold he certainly didn't tell me about it," Arabella said firmly. "Now let me out of here."

She stood up; and Descartes, unexpectedly, rose from his own seat and made a sweeping, bowing gesture towards the door as if inviting her to leave. She compressed her lips determinedly and marched to the door. Pancho had been watching the conversation, his piggy eyes darting from mouth to mouth; but now he became absorbed in an old penknife, its blade much worn and sharpened, which he was honing patiently with a stone.

"Do you mind?" Arabella demanded.

Pancho didn't move or look up.

"Our friend Pancho—he only lip-reads," Bernadotti remarked.

Arabella clicked her fingers repeatedly under his eyes; but still he didn't respond.

"It is not always easy to catch his attention," Descartes explained.

"I see," said Arabella slowly, as she turned back. "Perhaps if you . . . well, can you perhaps tell me a bit more about this money or gold, I'm supposed to know about?"

Suddenly, having edged into the middle of the room, she made a dash for the far door. But as she reached it, so did Pancho's knife. One second it wasn't there; the next, that well-worn blade was buried deep in the door, inches from her face.

She stared at the quivering knife and collapsed to a sitting posture on the floor, all the fight temporarily shaken out of her.

"If I knew where this gold was, I'd tell you," she pleaded helplessly.

Bernadotti stood up abruptly.

"Let's stop wasting time," he hissed. "We're gonna have to introduce you to some of our . . . livestock. The horned variety that helps people remember things they pretend they forgot, or that they pretend they never knew."

He laughed uproariously as his words sank in and Arabella turned several shades paler. He was still chuckling as, after two quick strides to reach her, he grasped her arm in a powerful and painful grip and propelled her towards the door.

"Let's go, Mrs high-class widow-lady. *Toro* is waiting for us!"

She searched Descartes' features hopefully for some sign of dissension in the camp. But his expression was stonily impassive, and she was led off with her arm in that pincer grip from the black-shirted and be-chained Bernadotti.

Thus is was that, not long after, Arabella Tatenor found herself in a bullring for the first time in her life.

It was a small bull-ring as bull-rings go, and clearly designed for training rather than public entertainment. But it did seem to possess most of the usual features—approximately circular, with a wooden perimeter, though with only a minimal two tiers of what would have been seating if actual seats had been present, and a few breaks around the circumference of the perimeter fence. There was the door she had been pushed through into the ring, a heavy iron latticework gate on the opposite side, and a similar gate at right angles to both. Only one conventional feature was lacking—and that deficiency, her hearing told her, was about to be remedied.

There was a bull, now revealed as big, black, and ugly, pawing the ground impatiently on the other side of the heavy iron gate facing her.

Descartes' voice floated fatly across to her.

"Have you decided to confide in us, Madame?"

Her eyes turned from side to side in despair and mute appeal.

"Please. Be reasonable. How can I tell you what I don't know?"

"I think you do know," came the fat voice. "And you will tell us—or else you are no further use to us. But you have very little time remaining."

There was a short pause followed by a

sharp mechanical click. The bull-gate swung slowly open.

Arabella pressed back against the fence behind in horror as the powerful snorting animal pushed its way through the gate. It trotted a few paces into the ring, and stopped. The morning sun reflected glossily off the perfect black muscularity of its back, and for a moment she was oddly, dispassionately aware of the beauty in that sheer animal power, before the parlousness of her own situation crowded in upon her again. She made a sudden panic-stricken dash for the door through which she had been propelled a minute before.

The bull lumbered into the middle of the ring, stopped, and seemed to see Arabella for the first time. He put his head down to charge. She rattled frantically at the door, tried to wrench it open by the heavy iron ring. It was locked. She hammered on it frenziedly with both fists.

"Let me out! *Let me out!*"

Descartes' voice carried across the ring again.

"The gold, Madame. For the last time, where is the gold?"

"For the last time," she gasped, *"I don't know."*

132

The bull began his charge towards her, and with a shriek she started to run along the perimeter fence. The bull turned to follow, began to bear down. She reversed direction and managed to increase her distance from the snorting animal, but then he skidded, turned, and came after her with renewed interest. She just succeeded in reaching a solitary board partition—a burladero shelter set close against the perimeter fence and threw herself behind its meagre protection.

The bull thundered headlong into the partition, hitting it from an oblique angle. It shuddered and shook, but held. And the bull drew back, cantering around in a tight circle for another assault as Arabella crouched terrified behind the board, which she could now see was rotten in parts.

"You can still be saved," came the voice of Descartes. "Quickly!"

Arabella saw that she had only one chance.

"All right, all right!" she gasped. "I'll tell you!"

But the bull had already begun to charge the board again. This time it crashed into it with frontal force. Some of the wood splintered away and those horns at their nearest were less than a foot and a half from where she crouched.

She heard the sounds of the door being unlocked—the door to at least temporary freedom. That last time-gaining bluff had been her only hope; she had only to invent some plausible location for the gold, which would have bought her a day or two in which, possibly, to find some other way out of this whole mess. But she had left it too late. She was trapped behind the burladero, and there was no way she could get to that door past the bull, which was already beginning the charge that would surely now take him through the rotting board which was her only remaining protection. All of this was borne in upon her, not by any calm process of ratiocination, but by the directly experienced realities of that September morning in the bull-ring of Jacques Descartes. There was the sun, not yet hot, but already warm as it climbed in the east; the dust of the ring; the snorting of the bull as it thundered towards her; the flimsy board that would not, could not, hold out. And most of all, there was the painful physical reality of that door to freedom only yards away; of the infinitely tantalising noise it had made, a rusty metallic scraping noise;

and of the fact that there was no way she would ever reach it.

And so she gave up the fight, stood up bravely, crossed her arms in front of her eyes, and waited for annihilation.

——4——

Arabella smelt the bull's hot breath, and heard the final splintering of the board which was all that stood between her and those lethal horns.

And in the same instant, and abruptly, she felt herself gripped by some altogether miraculous force that hoisted her straight up into the air, and she heard, as in a dream, the horns of the bull smashing into the perimeter fence only inches below the point in space where her feet now seemed to be dangling. After which the same miraculous force performed a second-stage hoist and she found herself standing on the first tier of the bull-ring stand, blinking at the realisation that she had just *not* been battered to smithereens.

"May I interest you in living?" enquired the miraculous force—which wore the outward semblance of Simon Templar.

Arabella was far too shaken and shattered and dumb-struck and relieved to attempt a reply. Besides which, even as she began to make sense of what had happened, she became more definitely aware that her escape was as yet far from being a complete *fait accompli*. An outraged bellowing from the opposite side of the ring reminded her that Descartes and the others were only yards away. Arabella made a feeble, dazed gesture towards the bellowing voices, and the Saint nodded.

"I think that's a very intelligent suggestion," he said earnestly. "Shall we?"

He grabbed her hand and jumped down the eight-foot drop off the outside of the bull-ring, from the upper tier, pulling her after him and helping to ease her landing. As they began to run, the bellowing crystallised itself into two urgent syllables in Descartes' voice.

"Get them!"

Simon and Arabella had only the few seconds' start given to them by the element of surprise. Simon knew they had to exploit that slender advantage for all it was worth; Arabella herself was in no state to know anything, and was more than content to take her cue from him. He paused just long enough to face her for a moment, with his hands on her shoulders and the gaze of his level blue eyes holding hers.

"Sorry, sweetheart," he said. "I know you've just had the scare of a lifetime, but now you're going to have to find the strength for the run of a lifetime." And then the Saint's long legs took him skimming across the stony courtyard with Arabella in tow, somewhat unsteadily on her shorter ones.

They made straight for the rough track leading to the main road. He had left his car about halfway along that track, well short of the *haras* itself, to be sure of making a discreet approach. Now, with several hundred yards between them and the Hirondel, he wished he had risked bringing it nearer.

As they sped past one side of a high-fenced corral, they caught a glimpse of Bernadotti and Pancho entering hurriedly by a gate on the other side. Within seconds they heard the sound of several sets of hooves giving chase behind them.

They glanced behind as they ran. Bernadotti, Pancho and another man, presumably one of the *haras* hands, were the pursuers. They were mounted on hefty picador horses; and they were armed with the murderous-looking eight-foot lances known as *pics*.

The Saint knew at once that they would not make it in a straight dash for the car. A lightning piece of strategic thinking was needed, and as usual when the chips were down, Simon Templar delivered.

He had three resources to work with, and he used them all to the full. The first was their lead, no more than thirty seconds, over the pursuers; the second was a godsent bend in the scrub-edged track; and the third was the rough mental map of the surrounding territory with which he had thoughtfully forearmed himself on his arrival.

As soon as they had rounded the bend and were out of sight, Simon ducked off into the narrow belt of scrub, still pulling Arabella by the hand.

"I'm afraid we're going to have to separate for a while," he told her in an urgent whisper, his mouth against her ear. "You'll have to decoy long enough for me to get to the car, farther along."

He pointed. She nodded her understanding, and he pointed again.

"Skirt the swamp, then strike back to the road."

"Swamp?" She silently mouthed the

word. Simon grinned and nodded. Then he picked up a large rock and lobbed it, in a high trajectory, into the undergrowth on the far side of the driveway. By now their mounted pursuers would have rounded the bend and realised that the fugitives had left the track.

They heard the horses take off after the sound of the falling rock, and Simon grinned again.

"The old tricks are sometimes the best." He signalled her to go; and she saw in his eyes that steely light of battle which many had seen before her, and many had feared, and some had loved. And then he was gone, like a fluid shadow melting into the undergrowth, and she found herself doing, almost automatically, what he had told her. She ran as quickly and noisily as she could out into the open and marshy terrain that bordered the *haras,* following a line away from the buildings but at an oblique angle to the track.

They heard her at once. Bernadotti and Pancho and the other man came crashing through the bushes on their powerful mounts. Arabella glanced behind as she ran. She had perhaps a fifty-yard advantage. She saw those great horses with their lanced riders thundering after her like some un-armoured jousters of a longpast age; and she ran as she had never run before.

The ground was rankly swampy with patches of somewhat higher grassy ground at intervals, and she found she could mostly judge her paces to land on these higher stepping-stones—whereas the horses were slowed somewhat by having to plunge and plop their way though the viscous ooze of the swamp. There were bushes and young trees at intervals, too, so that she followed a zigzag course in which pursuers and pursued lost sight of each other for a few seconds at a time.

But the snorting and splashing of the horses grew steadily louder, and she knew that they were inexorably catching her up. Then came the moment when she had to change direction and head for the track farther along, striking it, with luck, beyond the point where Simon should have rejoined his car.

If it had been only Bernadotti and Gomez pursuing, she would certainly have made it. But the other man was clearly a far better horseman; he was well ahead of them and now bearing down on her at speed.

She made the change of direction

abruptly, taking advantage of the cover given by some bushes. Still she heard the horses coming after her. But she heard another sound, too—one that sang in her ears as no sound of that kind ever had before.

It was the engine of the Saint's Hirondel springing into throbbing life.

Arabella made straight for it, the endurance of her legs and lungs now close to their limits. The car must be, from the sound, a good fifty yards away, and that horseman, with his *pic* poised, could be no more than a few paces behind her. And then, still running with a speed and surefootedness that astonished her, she was suddenly out of the swamp and back into that narrow strip of scrubby undergrowth bordering the track. She could feel her legs giving way as she ducked and swerved between the bushes in a last desperate endeavour to evade the thundering hooves and the murderous-looking lance. But the horseman crashed straight on through, simply flattening the bushes in his path.

Now she could see the car ahead, the engine still running . . .

And there was no one at the wheel.

The horseman was now so close behind that she could all but feel the point of the lance already impaling her through the small of her back. And then her legs buckled under her, and she tripped—exhausted, gasping, and covered in muddy slime. She must have passed out for a few moments; but through a kind of fog she heard a sharp *crack*, followed by the sort of heavy thud that might be made by a man falling off a horse.

The fog cleared, and she saw that a man had indeed fallen off a horse. And she saw Simon Templar standing in front of her, an automatic in his steady hand and a smile of admiration in his equally steady gaze.

Ten seconds later she found herself, somehow, in the passenger seat of the Hirondel and travelling rapidly towards the main road.

The Saint grinned at the pathetically dirty and dishevelled figure beside him, and wrinkled up his nose.

"Nice perfume," he remarked.

"Ho bloody ho!" she snorted, between gasping breaths. "Just *look* at me. And look at *you!* No dirt, no gook, no gunge—you're not even puffed!"

The Saint, cool and debonair, grinned again.

"Sorry. It was the only way. It was you

they wanted. They were bound to take off after you once they spotted you."

"But just *look* at me!" she repeated. She grabbed the driving mirror and turned it to gaze in horror at her face. "All my things, my bag—" She wailed: "—they're back there somewhere in my car. You found *me*. You could at least have found my bag."

"Oh, you're quite welcome," Simon said cheerfully. "Think nothing of it. I'm always saving people's lives."

She digested that for a while.

"I guess I *am* incredibly lucky you found me," she said finally, with conciliation in her voice. "But come to think of it, how on earth *did* you find me? What are you even *doing* in France, anyway?"

"Oh, you know, this and that," he told her. "I thought I'd see if I couldn't look up your husband's murderer."

"My husband's—murderer?" She looked at him aghast. "Are you mad? Is everybody mad?"

Simon recoiled fastidiously as she leaned rather too near. He waved her away.

"Uh . . . would you mind? I'm still fairly clean."

Her eyes blazed with anger at that.

"Yes, I sure damn well would mind," she

exploded. "And what on earth makes you think Charles was murdered?"

The Saint said: "There was a third person on the boat with him and Fournier. One who survived."

"And who was that third person?"

"That remains to be seen. But one thing we can be pretty certain of. Charles must have talked before he was killed. Otherwise he wouldn't have *been* killed. So, the survivor—the murderer—is at least one person who knows where the gold is."

"But how can you be so sure—" She stopped short, now very thoughtful. "Now *you're* talking about this 'gold'. Simon, how do you know all this? If Charles had some gold, how come they, and you, know all about it and *I* don't? And how come you were able to turn up back there, in the proverbial nick of time?" Arabella stopped again, with suspicion clouding her features. "What *is* all this, Simon? I can't even be sure of your part in it any more. So where's the nearest police station around here?"

The Saint sighed patiently.

"Dear lovely Arabella, you're understandably overwrought and suspicious, especially as I've had all the clean and heroic bits of the action today and you've had all the dirty,

144

dangerous and the strenuous ones. But wouldn't you like to know where there's several million dollars in gold bullion?"

"Several mill—" She sat back and thought for a minute, as they sped through the landscapes of southern France, now on the main road for Marseilles. Then, looking no less confused, she shrugged and said: "I could get used to bullion."

"Then you see why we're not going to the police just yet."

"I'm working on it."

"Plenty of time to think—while you're bathing."

After they had installed themselves in twin communicating suites in one of the better hotels of Marseille, Arabella lost no time in making the acquaintance of the bathroom, while Simon went out on a rapid shopping trip.

He came in carrying assorted feminine garments in both the under- and the outer-wear categories, as well as sundry toiletries. There was no end to the surprising range of knowledge he had picked up in his adventurer's life, and the fact that he was capable of choosing well-matched feminine accoutrements to suit a woman's taste should occasion neither surprise nor indelicate enquiry.

He dropped the clothing on the bed and knocked on the door of Arabella's bathroom, from which issued forth exuberant sounds of splashing.

"All right if I come in? I promise not to look. Unless you insist, of course."

He went in, face half-averted.

"It doesn't matter," she said. "You can look."

Simon looked.

She was lying in a bath full of completely opaque brownish liquid covered with suds.

"Lovely, isn't it? Like Lake Erie."

"Anything you find in there," he said gravely, as he deposited some appropriate toiletries on the end of the bath, "—spray it with this. Or better yet, you might let that water out before you take root."

As she turned to go, she called out softly.
"Simon?"

"Yes?"

"You're a very attractive man."

The Saint grinned, and indicated the bath water.

"I'm the one who should be doing the flattering—you filthy rich widow, you. I almost wish we were here for a dirty week-

146

end instead of on dangerous business." His face was suddenly serious and intent. "You've been through enough already to know that gold, in the quantities we're talking about, is *very* dangerous business. Make no mistake—Descartes and his less philosophical cronies aren't going to give up easily. Don't run away with the idea, even when you finally get out of that water, that we've got clean away from them."

Even as the author of this paronomastic caution, Simon was unaware of quite how timely it was. For as he drove away from the hotel shortly after, he was observed from a black Citroen that lurked not fifty yards along the street. The obese body of Jacques Descartes oozed comfortably across the back seat, while in the front Enrico Bernadotti and Pancho Gomez exchanged small smiles of satisfaction as the Hirondel disappeared around the next corner.

IV: How Inspector Lebec introduced Himself, and Captain Finnegan accepted Coffee.

—1—

The Marseille harbourmaster was regretful but definite.

"No, Monsieur. There has been no such vessel in the Marina here during the last two months." He stabbed a broad sunburned hand at the record-book that lay open on his desk. "You see—in July, she left her berth here, without disclosing any destination." He shrugged. "We have no powers to require that, you understand. Perhaps Cannes, or Nice, or San Tropez. I am sorry, but the yacht *Phoenix* is nowhere in the port of Marseille."

It had been Simon's idea to get out of the way while Arabella was completing her resanitisation in the hotel. During the latter part of the drive from the *haras* after their hurried escape, she had already sketched in the missing details for him, as much as she had gleaned from the solicitor. That included her current financial status and absolute need to sell a yacht whose existence she had hitherto never even suspected. And the obvious first step for the Saint had been to go out and find that yacht, the more so as he had also been told about Charles Tatenor's twice-yearly disappearances followed by periods of evident renewed solvency. Fairly obviously, there might well be a link between the *Phoenix* and those regular and lucrative vanishing acts.

The immediate problem now was to locate the *Phoenix*. And that was a task which the harbourmaster's negative news did nothing to simplify.

Simon Templar's mind was thoughtfully absorbed with this new and unforeseen problem as he made his way back to the hotel, and he had parked his car and almost reached the hotel entrance before he saw Arabella's MG. It was at the kerbside behind a police car, and Arabella herself was standing beside it looking decidedly fetching in some of her new clothes. She was not alone; there were three men with her. One was instantly recognisable as a uniformed policeman, and the other two were just as instantly recognisable as plainclothes policemen. The taller of these possessed a shock of white hair and the shorter an air of relative seniority. Some photographs were spread out on the low roof of Arabella's car, and the senior-looking policeman was speaking.

". . . and all of these five men, Madame, including your husband, were involved in the theft of valuable cargo passing from Marseille to Morocco . . ."

"About five million dollars' worth of gold bars, wasn't it?" said the Saint chattily as he ambled up to join the group.

The speaker turned, and looked at Simon with almost transparent fishlike grey-green eyes in a face that was alert yet slightly pudgy. His mouth had that peculiarly Gallic impassivity which, it is said, is conferred only by long years of drinking pastis and pretending to like it.

"I am Inspector Gérard Lebec," he said rapidly. "And you—you would be Monsieur Simon Templar—who has travelled here with this lady to *find* that gold."

"No!" Arabella protested. "We didn't even travel together. And we don't know about any gold. At least, *I* don't . . ."

Her voice trailed off, and Lebec pounced on the note of uncertainty.

"You perhaps do not, Madame. But Mr Templar knows—oh yes, *he* knows! Are you aware, Madame Tatenor, that there was a *sixth* man in the stealing of that gold?"

Arabella shook her head slowly.

"I didn't even know there were five . . . I mean until recently I'd never *heard* of the robbery at all."

"Ah, but yes." Lebec turned the cold transparent eyes on the Saint again while continuing to address his remarks ostensibly to Arabella. "He was, it is said, a man working on the Moroccan side, and known only to your husband."

"Yes, Inspector," Simon said with good-humoured patience. "I *have* been to Morocco."

"And would it not be this man number six," Lebec persisted, "who murdered your husband at the boat race . . . supposing it to have been murder?"

"Yes, Inspector," the Saint put in, "I *was* in that boat race."

Arabella glanced from Simon to Lebec and back to Simon.

"This is nonsense—isn't it?" she said to Simon. And then to Lebec: "I happen to admire and trust Mr Templar very much . . . At least, I think I do."

Lebec's lips curled in contempt, as again he looked at Simon but spoke to Arabella.

"Your own Scotland Yard does not share your confidence. Nor do we, nor Interpol nor half the police forces of the world."

Simon smiled his most impudent police-baiting smile.

"With my first conviction coming here and now, I take it?"

At that Lebec's manner froze over completely. He made a point of bowing curtly to Arabella and not looking further at the Saint.

"I may wish to interview you again," he told her. "Meanwhile you will both please not to depart Marseille without my permission. *Au revoir*, Madame."

He gestured to his tall white-haired colleague and the uniformed man with a crisp *"Allons,"* and they drove off in the police car, leaving Arabella looking decidedly thoughtful.

It was clear that Lebec's words had refuelled her uncertainties, if not exactly suspicions, about the Saint's own interest in the affair of the gold—which, infuriatingly to her, everyone seemed to know about with the exception of herself.

She told him that the police had found her car abandoned on the main road outside the village, and that the papers they found

152

in it had eventually enabled them to trace her through the hotel registration. Then she asked, almost absent-mindedly:

"Did you find the *Phoenix?*"

Simon told her the harbourmaster's bad news. But it had less impact on her than expected. She had been through enough of a shock to her way of life recently, he supposed; she was almost resigned to expecting that things would go wrong at every turn.

"But it *has* to be there," she said without much conviction. "I mean, that's the only reason I'm . . . Anyway, how *do* you know all about the bullion and these men, and Charles, and all?"

"I have a friend in high places," he said. "And that's the truth."

Later, more from a need of breathing-space than in any positive hope of locating the elusive *Phoenix,* they wandered along by the magnificent private-yacht harbour in the dying sunshine of a matchless September evening.

"I don't even know what she looks like," Arabella lamented. "It seems quite hopeless, doesn't it? Anyway, we can surely believe the harbourmaster if he says she's not here. Or is he involved too?" She eyed the Saint quizzically. "Maybe you think *he's* the sixth man."

"Stranger things have happened," said the Saint, whose thoughts at the time, if the truth be told, were mostly preoccupied with the logistics of making himself and Arabella vanish at the right moment from the sight of the tall white-haired shadow who had been lurking at a not quite discreet enough distance behind them since the start of the evening's expedition.

It was not that Simon Templar had any immediate plans to get up to anything nefarious, or which he would otherwise not wish Inspector Lebec or one of Lebec's men to observe. But the Saint did have a rooted dislike of being followed about.

Doubtless there exists, in some shadier nook or cranny of Whitehall's less public departments, or their equivalents in other countries, an official but restricted manual codifying the various available manoeuvres for shaking off a professional shadow; and it may be that item 17.3b/1 therein treats of the timely interposition of visually obstructive obstacles and of making a rapid alteration of pedestrian course under cover of such an obstacle. But to the Saint's thought processes, which dealt with the world in as direct and tangible a way as they could, it was a simple, enjoyable and uncluttered matter. You waited till something got in the way between you and the shadow, and then you dodged off niftily in the opposite direction. Ideally, to complete the enjoyment you then found a vantage point from which you could watch the shadow stumble around scratching his head, wondering where on earth you had vanished to.

In this instance, a longish sailing-craft which was being slowly pushed along the wharf on a dray supplied the obstacle. Simon chose his moment to place himself and Arabella on the opposite side of it from the white-haired detective, and then he cut rapidly back, dragging her into a narrow alleyway between wharfside yacht chandleries, and thence via some steps to a tiny buvette, from a back window of which they had a good but discreet view below, and they watched Lebec's man as he figuratively, if not actually, scratched his head for a while before he finally gave up and went away.

Later that night, after a leisurely dinner, they still had to admit that they were no farther forward with the problem of locating the *Phoenix*. As there seemed nothing constructive to do for the moment, a look at the nightlife, with some appropriate unwinding, seemed as good an idea as any. No doubt they would have the white-haired detective or his replacement trailing along behind; but that at least offered the optional entertainment of shaking him off again if all else proved tedious; though it might not be so easy next time. They drove to the Club Bidou, which was recommended by the hotel's friendly reception staff.

Named after a traditional provençal bar-counter dice game, it was a drink-and-dance club where the décor was based on mirrors repeating every image to infinity, the style was excuse-me, and the table cloths were symbolically green-baize plastic. At the entrance there were shelves full of semitransparent plastic cubes with dice markings, large enough to fit over a reveller's head and be kept in place by wire clips inside, providing complete anonymity from the neck up. Thus, unexpectedly, Simon Templar became for a time a blue "six" and Arabella a pink "three".

Two drinks later, they were enjoying some energetic dancing when abruptly the music changed to a samba, and a buxom red "two" tapped the Saint on the shoulder and danced away with him. While he was trying to disengage himself with reasonable civility, Arabella found herself grabbed by a green "five." She could see little of him in the dim lighting, but what was visible of his dark clothing below the mask made her uneasy, for no reason she could immediately put her finger on.

Then, as they moved around and the light glanced on his torso, she stifled a gasp. He was wearing a black shirt, open almost to the waist, and on his chest a gold chain glinted as it caught the light.

The green cube leaned close.

"Where is the gold?" hissed Bernadotti's voice.

He tilted back his mask-helmet and stared hard at her in the half-light. The wolfish white teeth flashed briefly. She wrenched herself away, tried to run—only to find her way barred by a grotesque Tweedledum figure.

"Where is the gold?" whispered Descartes, raising his mask.

She turned to run the other way—and was promptly grabbed by a shorter man who tilted his cube to reveal the blubbery lips of Pancho Gomez. Frenzied, she somehow managed to tear herself from the nightmarish trio, who were trying to hem her in.

She slipped away under the outstretched arm of Bernadotti and almost threw herself upon a nearby blue "six."

"Simon! Simon it's *them!* They're here!"

The "six" said nothing, but leaned heavily against her.

"Simon, did you hear me? It's . . ."

Her voice tailed away as the "six" slumped forward, revealing a slim dagger buried between his shoulderblades.

—2—

Arabella gasped and jumped back. The "six" crashed to the ground and lay still. The dancers spread back, clearing a space around the fallen man. The music came, it seemed unwillingly, to a halt.

Then someone bent down and took off the "six" helmet. It was not the Saint. It was the white-haired detective. That was too much for Arabella. She fainted dead away—only to be deftly caught by a man who had pushed through the crowd from behind. He raised his "six" cube. It was the Saint. He patted her face to revive her, at the same time gazing intently around the room.

One of the dancers, a man, was sliding

around the back of the crowd, making quietly for the exit.

Arabella opened her eyes.

"Welcome back," Simon said as, supporting her, he hustled her after the man.

"Simon—I thought it was you!" she said weakly.

He nodded grimly.

"So did someone else."

As they emerged into the street, a small blue van was just moving off some twenty or thirty yards away. In the available light it was impossible to get any view of the driver's face, but within seconds they were following in the Hirondel.

The driver of the van had just a fraction too much of a start: he made turn after rapid turn, down ever narrower sidestreets—a type of driving in which a car the size of the Hirondel could hardly be at its best, even with the formidable skill of a Simon Templar behind the wheel. Inevitably, there came a time when Simon had to come to a screeching halt for a party of inebriates crossing the road just after the van had sped around a corner ahead of them and out of sight; and then they lost it.

Simon drove on for a while, filling the air with half-silent objurgations. All he had left that was worth trying was to continue, not very hopefully, in the same rough general direction the van had taken so far. Working on that admittedly hit-or-miss principle, in due course they emerged into a wider street, a dimly lit dock service road of some kind. He drove on slowly for a minute or two, peering into the pools of darkness on either side. He was about to give it up as a bad job when Arabella suddenly tugged at his sleeve.

"Simon—look!"

He looked where she was pointing. In the light of the half-moon, they could just make out the shape of a small van, parked in a narrow side street alongside a high dock wall.

They got out, and approached the van cautiously. It was blue, and the engine felt warm, but nobody was inside. They looked around, their eyes becoming accustomed to the dark. On one side of the narrow bend was some waste ground strewn with rubble; on the other, the high dock fence, unbroken by any gate or opening, as far as could be seen. Then Simon spotted what might, at a stretch, have been called an opening—just a narrow vertical slot where one plank was missing.

He tested an adjacent plank and found it

loose. He took it out, and they squeezed silently through the gap. Once through, they paused on the other side of the fence, listening. Ahead of them, nothing; behind, only a couple of car engines playing their gearbox tunes somewhere on the night air.

Simon led the way as they advanced stealthily down a path which in due course took them to a gap between two warehouse-like buildings. His acute hearing picked up a faint shuffling sound, and what might have been humming, from some distance ahead; and it was because he was concentrating on that more distant sound, and trying to analyse it, that he almost missed the nearer one until it was too late.

Near the gap between the two buildings was a pile of crates, just visible in the moonlight, and it was from the upper area of this heap of crates that the scraping, creaking sound came. A half second later, a huge crate came crashing down, almost on top of him. It was only that preliminary creaking, as the crate teetered on the brink before it fell, that saved him. It gave him the split second that was all his highly tuned reflexes needed, and he sprang back, and suffered nothing worse than a bruised toe as the big crate jarred against his foot on its way down.

For long moments the Saint stood stock still, and Arabella did likewise, while they listened for any sound following that tremendous crash. But they heard nothing from the immediate vicinity—only, from time to time, the strange shuffling and humming, or crooning, from some distance ahead, that Simon had heard before.

They went on warily, skirting the fallen crate, then passing between the buildings and circumnavigating various pieces of heavy marine equipment and fittings. The sounds were louder now, and there could be no doubt that the crooning, or babbling, was human. It was therefore no real surprise when, a little while after, as they neared a dark corrugated iron fence, the shuffling materialised out of the darkness as a man-shaped apparition that sang, if that is the word:

"Too-Ra-Loo-Ra-Loo-Ral,
"Too-Ra-Loo-Ra-Loi-ee,
"Too-Ra-Loo-La . . . Roo-Ra . . .
Roora . . . "

The confused singing trailed off into muttered unintelligible cursing as the man came to a shambling halt at the corrugated iron fence. For a minute or so he seemed at a loss to know what to make of the obstacle. Then a brilliant idea seemed to strike him, and he steadied himself against the fence with one hand while the other fumbled with something that jangled like a bunch of keys, that defeated his befuddled fingers for another minute or so. Then he apparently managed to select a key and, after further painfully protracted endeavours, opened a flush-fitting door in the fence. He lurched through, with the Saint and Arabella following at a distance. They saw him pause and take a long swig from a king-sized hip-flask. There followed an audible smacking of the lips, after which the slurred travesty of singing was resumed.

> *Ooh-ver in . . .Kill-llarney,*
> Many-y yea-rrs a-gooh,
> Me moddh-horr sang dhis . . .

As the man stumbled on into the gloom, Simon and Arabella both pulled up dead at the same instant.

There on the left, looming above them, were the gleaming white bows of a luxury yacht. Even in that limited moonlight, the large gilt lettering of the name on her bow was unmistakable.

It was the *Phoenix*.

"Dry dock!" Simon said softly. "No wonder we couldn't find her!"

"But she's *beautiful!*" Arabella exclaimed in wonderment. There was a sudden rustle of sound behind them, and the Saint whirled as Inspector Lebec stepped through the doorway in the fence.

"She is indeed beautiful," he agreed crisply. "But it may be many years, unfortunately, before either of you will be at liberty to enjoy her. Which should at least put an end to the activities of Monsieur Simon Templar!"

Lebec had an automatic levelled, and the two detectives who followed close behind him were similarly equipped, and appeared similarly in earnest.

"Hands raised!" Lebec commanded tautly. "Up! Behind the neck!"

They complied slowly, Simon sighing inaudibly as he did so at Lebec's having so quickly lived up to his earlier promised nuisance value.

"May I enquire, Inspector," he asked lazily, "what crime we are supposed to have committed? Is my car parked on a blue line, perhaps?"

"You are both under arrest for the murder of a police officer at the Club Bidou one half hour ago," said Inspector Lebec.

—3—

The Marseille police headquarters building in those days was a monolithic greystone structure of undistinguished frontage. From the outside, the cells could be identified from their windows, which were smaller than the others and fitted with bars in the time-honoured fashion. There was, in short, nothing outwardly remarkable about the building, as police headquarters go. Nevertheless it had just earned a coveted distinction which few other such establishments had yet managed to achieve, despite keen international competition for the honour.

One of its cells had just housed Simon Templar overnight.

It was a point of pride with the Saint, as well as a mark of his care, foresight and resourcefulness, that he had never yet been convicted of any criminal offence in any country. Over the years, he had grown used to the efforts of zealous and overzealous policemen, most of whom dreamed of rectifying the omission and yearned obsessively to shut the notorious Saint away behind bars for a good long stretch. Every so often, one would manage to detain him for a while on some tenuous ground which owed more to desperate policemanly optimism than to any hard evidence of law-breaking on the part of the Saint. That Simon Templar frequently broke the law is, in a chronicle of strict truth, undeniable; but the circumstances in which he broke it, and his choice of victims upon whom to visit his sometimes violent notions of poetic justice, were such that no hard evidence could be mustered as a basis for holding him.

However, there were admittedly times when Simon Templar lost patience with the petty authoritarian behavior of some idiotic sergeant or inspector; and those were the occasions when he sometimes yielded to the temptation to pull strings in order to speed up his inevitable release. He had his powerful friends and contacts even in certain police forces around the world. For there had been times, and would continue to be times, when the aims of the Saint and those of the law were not incompatible; and many a police officer had cause to be grateful for Simon Templar's timely intervention.

One such contact came to mind on this occasion. He was Pierre Duport, a high-ranking officer of the Sûreté in Nice, whose name was respected in police circles the length of the Riviera. Duport owed him at least a small favour in return for the Saint's part, two years before, in the affair of a certain Corsican chemist found trussed up like a turkey outside Duport's office, his shaven head branded indelibly with the descriptive words *marchand de stupéfiants*.

But the Saint had hesitated—knowing Duport's nocturnal inclinations—to attempt to trace him at two in the morning. Judging from Lebec's manner, a night in the cells was in any case a certainty, come what might, for both him and Arabella.

In the morning, and before any formal charges had been laid, he had no hesitation in claiming his right to a telephone call and in using it to make contact with Duport. He outlined the problem tersely, and Duport immediately undertook to telephone Lebec's superiors and explain to them in the strongest as well as the simplest terms that Monsieur Simon Templar, whatever else he might have done in his unorthodox life, did not kill policemen on such slender acquaintance.

The call must have had its effect; for less than an hour later the two of them were brought before a strangely subdued Lebec.

"I am very sorry your man is dead, Inspector," Simon told him. "Unfortunately he was wearing a mask identical to mine, and we're of similar height. Obviously someone thought he was me."

"Indeed?" Lebec said without conviction. He returned to his previous practice of addressing himself primarily to Arabella. "Whether Monsieur Templar was the target intended, is perhaps open for debate, which I do not propose to enter. It is enough that there is confirmation of your story from several of the other dancers. Nobody observed the stabbing." Lebec sniffed disdainfully, as if utterly unwilling to be convinced himself by what he was saying. "Therefore, nobody saw who wielded the knife. Therefore, I must release you both." He bowed slightly to Arabella. "In your case, Madame, it is a pleasure. In the case of Monsieur Templar, a great regret."

"I love you too, Gérard," said the Saint.

Lebec got up from his chair and moved

168

around on the desk to sit, less formally, on its edge.

"Madame—a few words of friendly advice. Already you have spent a night in the police cell. I regret any discomfort—which, I suggest, you would not have risked but for travelling with this notorious criminal Templar. Be very careful with this man, Madame. I have told you of the gold robbery—and of the sixth man. Your husband alone knew his identity."

"Inspector Lebec," Arabella said loyally. "I think you ought to stop intimating that Simon is that man."

"Thanks, sweetheart," Simon put in with a brief baring of the teeth. "That's one I owe you. Don't let me forget it."

"But I put it to you, Madame," Lebec persisted, "that if he *is* the sixth man, he will be as merciless with you as with the other three survivors who already seek the gold."

Simon yawned elaborately and twiddled his thumbs.

"May we please go, Inspector? It really is very boring in here. Something to do with the conversation."

Lebec nodded stiffly and showed them out, though not without repeating his earlier instruction that they were to report to him before leaving Marseille.

There was no need for them to discuss where they were going. Only breakfast might have stood between them and an exploration of the *Phoenix;* and breakfast, of a kind, they had been given at the police station.

One of Lebec's men had nervously driven the Hirondel over from the dock area where it had been left, and now the Saint drove back there and found the orthodox entrance to the dry dock where they had seen the *Phoenix.*

During the drive, he was conscious of some sidelong and quizzical glances from his passenger. Lebec's words, it seemed, had re-watered the small seed of doubt which had already threatened to burgeon into full-blown mistrust once before, after their first meeting with the Inspector. Arabella was turning over past events in her mind, comparing what she knew of Simon from personal acquaintance—in truth not a great deal—with the scenario Lebec had implied. But Simon said nothing; he knew that Arabella would surface with her own conclusions or questions, or challenges, when she was good and ready, and it would have gained him nothing to have broached the matter again himself there and then.

The *Phoenix*, to Arabella's delight, was exactly as they had seen her. If anything she was even more impressive in daylight. She was a beautiful hundred-footer, her hull and superstructure gleaming with new white paint. For a minute or two Arabella just stood and gawped; then she walked up and down and gawped some more from several different angles for another minute or two. There was no one in sight.

"Well," she said finally, "what are we waiting for? Let's go aboard."

There was silence as they crossed a gangway to the main deck. Simon kept his eyes skinned, and his muscles were alert for instant action. He hadn't forgotten the fugitive of the night before, he who had driven the van; and neither had he forgotten the strange freak of chance—if that was what it was—that had caused a crate to fall at the very instant when he was about to walk under it.

There was no sign of anyone on deck. They opened the door to the main saloon and went in. It was lavishly appointed, with heavy ornate furniture and an apparently well-stocked bar; but dominating the room

171

was a hugh oil painting on the far wall, a portrait of the familiar face of Charles Tatenor—an almost photographic likeness of the man, complete with yachting cap.

"Cha—" Arabella began in an automatic exclamation, but Simon put his finger to his lips warningly. His acute hearing had picked up the faintest susurration from somewhere within the accommodation. He led the way silently through a teak door in the after bulkhead, and then along a short passageway. The noise was louder there, and increased still more as they approached a door marked "Galley" at the end of the passageway.

Suddenly there was a crash from within. The Saint wrenched open the door—and almost tripped over an empty bottle.

It was a bottle that had held Irish whiskey.

And on his knees, and held upright only by the counterweight of one arm slung across the galley stove, was a middle-aged, very Irish-looking, very drunk-looking, disheveled and unshaven man, who had yet managed somehow, through all that, to keep his gold-braided cap on.

". . . second thoughts, I think I'll rest in me cabin," he muttered; and the voice was instantly recognisable as that of the tipsy crooner from the night before. He was now, if anything, drunker than he had been then. Even as they watched, his eyes glazed and he toppled over on his face.

Arabella looked at Simon, then at the inert figure, which had begun to snore, then back at Simon.

"What are we going to do with *him?*"

"I suppose," Simon mused, "we'd better have a shot at bringing him round, so that we can try to figure out who he is and what he's doing here. Do you suppose there's any coffee in the place that isn't eighty proof?"

It took an hour of repeated cold-water treatments, after the Saint had heaved him into a chair, before the man recovered enough to make any semblance of sense. Now half-awake, he spluttered through the black coffee that Arabella was pouring determinedly into his unwilling mouth.

"Every drop of it, Captain," said the Saint, who had been thumbing through the ship's log. "I take it you *are* what's left of Captain William Finnegan?"

"Wha—. . . ? How . . . ? Who . . . ? Where . . . ?" He glowered at Simon. "None of your damn business. Get off me ship, the pair of yous."

He grimaced at the taste of the coffee and clamped his jaws firmly shut against any further incursions of the vile non-alcoholic liquor.

To Arabella, the Saint said: "You can pour that coffee *in* or *on* him." And to Finnegan. "Your choice, Cap'n. Now—we followed someone here last night driving a blue van. Do you drive a blue van?"

Finnegan tried unsteadily to rise to his feet. He was a big burly man, his dark hair flecked with grey, his eyes bloodshot.

"I'll drive *you* right over the side, you—"

He never completed the appellation, because at that moment Arabella calmly poured most of a cup of hot coffee over his head. Finnegan howled and spluttered in inebriate rage, then sank back in his seat and stared up at Arabella with a kind of awestruck respect. She returned the stare with innocent aplomb. Finnegan continued, with an intermittent half-fearful glance in her direction.

"A van? I couldn'ta navigated a pram last night. I was after goin' to a little drinkin' party along the harbour a way, d'ye see."

"Whose party?" Simon queried.

"Old Michael—Michael Jardine, the chan-

174

dler fella. He's the one stocked me up for the cruise. Only . . ."

"What about the cruise?"

"Aw—it's off now. The owner died, you know. Mr Charles. Mr Charles Tatenor."

"Go on."

"Well—sure and I'm jest waitin' for me instructions now. The lawyers, y'know." He shook his head. "Sad business it is. We had some good times, Mr Charles and me. Coupla times a year, sailing away south, cruisin' and all."

"And all?" The Saint's interest had hardened and he came close to fix the still-groggy Finnegan with a firm cynical eye. "Cruising and *what?*"

Finnegan took on a dreamy look.

"Cruisin' and fishin'—and kissin' the girls. Great feller he was."

"A couple of times a year, you say. Where did you go on these trips?"

"Kissing *what* girls?" Arabella put in before Finnegan could get focused on the Saint's question.

"First stop was always Corsica. Same little bay, every time. Gem of an island, that."

"*What* girls?" Arabella shouted; and Finnegan jumped up out of the chair in such alarm that he moved with almost sober alacrity.

"The woman's mad, I tell you, mad. Get her off me ship this very minute!"

"Actually, Captain," Simon told him, "it's *her* ship. Captain Finnegan—Mrs Charles Tatenor."

Finnegan digested this in stunned silence for a long minute. Then he got up, went close to her and inspected her at close quarters, with evident approval. Then he finally broke out with a broad grin, as if at a long-lost daughter.

"Well, if that isn't . . . ! Well, now! Mrs Charles indeed! And a fine tough-minded woman you are, m'dear." An even broader grin now split his stubbed face from ear to ear. He extended his hand and pumped hers warmly.

"Captain," said the Saint. "The logbook says the drydock work's completed. How soon can you have her in the water?"

Finnegan was still concentrating his attention on Arabella, now with a warm and admiring deference.

"Missus," he said in reply to Simon's question, "you gimme t'ree hours after you pay them bloodsucking drydock book accountants, and I'll have her bobbin' on the waves."

"After *I* pay—" Arabella gasped.

"Dry-dock charges will be paid today, Captain," Simon told him calmly.

"They will?" said Arabella.

"We want to be under way by late afternoon. On the same course you would have taken with Charles Tatenor."

4

When the Saint got back to the hotel that afternoon, he found Arabella with her red leather suitcase and matching vanity bag packed and waiting alongside his own luggage which he had seen to earlier.

He brandished a receipted bill.

"The *Phoenix*'ll be ready when we are."

She eyed the receipt, moved up close to take it from him—and pecked him on the cheek.

"Simon," she said seriously, "it's incredibly generous of you to—" Her eyes grew wide and round as she read the amount. "Good Lord! Did they fix it or line it with—bullion? You paid *this?*"

Simon submitted to another kiss without protest.

"Be careful," he told her. "I might get a taste for it . . . Your solicitor told you that Charles paid his bills after walking in with great lumps of money twice a year. Well, twice a year he took the *Phoenix* out with Finnegan. So, we go where they went."

Arabella looked again at the bill.

"But at these prices—why, you have to be either very rich or . . . hoping to get very rich."

"I was hoping for a little sea air, actually," Simon told her innocently. And that light of Saintly mockery she had seen before glinted in his eyes again as he reached down for her luggage.

Arabella stopped him, and searched his features for a few moments with an intent seriousness.

"Simon, *were* you that sixth man? You could have been."

"I could," said the Saint. "But I wasn't."

"But it's the way you live, the way you've lived for a long time, isn't it? A gold bullion robbery—it's something you easily *could* have been involved with. And don't tell me you never worked with others. You used to have—a sort of gang, once, so I read."

178

Simon laughed gently.

"Yes, but those were other days, and that was another Simon Templar." For a moment the eyes of the maturer Simon Templar were clouded with recollections of those vanished years. "That was a long time ago," he told her.

"Well, if you're not the sixth man, why can't you take me, and Inspector Lebec for that matter, into your confidence . . . ? Well, okay, I guess I can see why you hold out on him. But I have a feeling you're holding out on me too, damn it. You held out on me back on the island. Simon, I've trusted you. I *am* trusting you, or trying to." She looked levelly at him. "Why can't you trust me?"

"Because," said the Saint, leaning closer and closer as she finished speaking, "you have . . . very . . . shifty eyes."

And being now well within the accepted distance for such things, he kissed her gently.

Flippancy was the response that arose in him most immediately and automatically in the face of a question he was instinctively reluctant to explore in any serious depth. Had he been analytically inclined in these matters, Simon Templar might have had to

179

confess to himself that perhaps he had needed to maintain some space between the two of them, figuratively speaking, because the simple fact was that she had affected him more than any other woman he had met in a long time; and the Saint was, by established professional habit, wary of any involvement that might carry even a hint of jeopardising the "free" in his freebootery.

He had not worked it out in so many words in the case of Arabella, but the fact was that freedom was an inseparable element of his life and character. He had been his own unique globetrotting blend of pirate and adventurer for enough years now to know that he would go on in the same freewheeling ways as long as there was still strength in his body and a new vista of ungodliness over the next hill.

That was how it was with the Saint, just as for others life might be inconceivable except as a doctor or chartered accountant or in any of a thousand other worthy and stable roles. The Saint saw the necessity for these, and was grateful that others wanted to occupy themselves thus, and to lead conventional and settled lives, leaving him to live out his own notions of buccaneering chivalry and justice for as long as it pleased him; to ride the high winds of adventure, changing little with the seasons or the years; here and there dipping into new valleys, fighting new battles, or fighting again the old ones under new skies; but always, and above all, remaining free.

He had the potential to settle to a humdrum existence like any other man; but it remained a potential, like that of a winged seed staying always aloft.

Those who had worked with him, that select handful of men, and one woman, who had shared his ideals all those long years ago—his "gang" as Arabella had called them—they had once been the same, and had floated as free. But one by one, when their time had come, they had ceased to float, and had dropped to the ground, and put down roots, and settled.

Once, such a precarious and fateful time of choice had come for Simon Templar also, when he found himself poised in the air, becalmed; and it was with a great emptiness, at the time, that he had chosen as he knew he had been fated to choose from the beginning, and had watched as the person for whom he would have given up anything but his destiny, and who understood that as

181

well as he did himself, went on her golden way.

And so he had continued to follow his own star as the years had rolled on; and if he had his way he would be doing so still in as many more years hence. It seemed as likely that the earth might stop, as that there would one day cease to be villains abroad and booty to be won—or, as in the present case, bullion to be grabbed, if the gods were willing, from under the noses of the villains.

And it was because of all this, which was unspoken, that the Saint had covered a hiatus with a flippant comment, and had kissed Arabella Tatenor before picking up her luggage and taking it out of the hotel with his own.

They were met by Finnegan as they boarded the *Phoenix*. But this was a very different Finnegan from the one they had seen before. Here was a tough old sea-dog—flinty-eyed, observant, exuding competence from the peaked cap down. His expression was serious and businesslike.

"Welcome aboard to you both." He shook hands warmly with them. "Got no other hands for you, though."

"And if you was-a me, you'd be pretty damned careful, huh?" said the Saint, parodying Bernadotti's Italo-American accent as he glanced behind to confirm the presence of Pancho. And to him, he said: "Now you won't be a silly boy with that thing, will you?"

At a nod from Descartes, Pancho slid forward and frisked Simon expertly. Having found nothing, he was preparing to turn his attention to a still-incredulous Arabella, but Descartes signalled him to stop.

"If Monsieur Templar has no gun, I think we can assume the lady is also unarmed." He inclined his head in a half-bow to Arabella. "Madame, we regret the intrusion upon your boat. But you must remember, our claim is older than yours. Your Charles, he owed us a great deal, which he had not paid at the time of his death. This boat, indeed, would not have been bought, I think, except for the gold which your Charles—our Karl—kept entirely for himself."

"The lady told you before," Simon said with steel in his voice. "She doesn't know about any gold."

Descartes nodded.

"It is another regret that we did not accept her statement. Perhaps, after all, he did *not* share with her the secret . . . the secret which lies, does it not Monsieur Templar, in the voyages of the *Phoenix?*"

"And what did you threaten Captain Finnegan with?" Simon enquired evenly.

The reply, an evil grin and a throat-cutting mime, came from Bernadotti.

"He would have gone the same way you're gonna go, Templar. To feed the sharks."

"Nice to know you're feeling really hospitable," Simon observed. "What a pity your chum Tranchier can't be here to complete the party. He'd have made it a quartet of physical repulsiveness. But I must say you three do get around—for a bunch of farmers."

"Who's looking after the pigs?" Arabella put in, having now partly adjusted her mind to the new development and the uncomfortable fact that the visitors were with them for the time being whether she liked it or not.

Descartes' eyes blazed with anger and his voice cut across the room like the crack of a whip.

"We are not farmers! And we have no pigs! We are very seriously seeking that gold—and we will have it!" He fixed them both for a few moments. Then, ticking off

186

the items on his fingers as he spoke, he added: "To save for you the trouble, we have smashed the radio—broken the signal lamps—thrown overboard the rifle—even the axe for fires. So—be at home with us."

The Saint considered the invitation dispassionately and nodded to its reasonableness. He took Arabella's arm and led her to some vacant chairs.

"Scotch and water, please," he said expectantly.

"Gin and tonic—with ice," Arabella added.

"Get it yourself!" growled Bernadotti.

Two hours and perhaps three or four spaced-out drinks later, Simon was just beginning yet another game of backgammon with Descartes, who had been animated by the play to a new exuberance of mood in which all other preoccupations were for the time forgotten.

"Finally, I have met a worthy opponent. Not for nothing am I titled, among the French players, *Jacques du trictrac.*"

"I've heard the name," Simon lied, having seen at a very early stage of the proceedings that his reasonable knowledge of the game could be a valuable asset in dealing with Descartes.

"Monsieur Templar, you play very skill-fully the difficult retarded game," Descartes declared. "Have you read the Schneider book, by chance?"

The Saint hadn't, but he had heard of the Austrian who was generally regarded as the best player in Europe.

"I've played a game or two with old Rudy," he said casually.

"Played? You have actually played with Schneider?"

Simon smiled as he "captured" one of Descartes' pieces and transferred it to the bar.

"Only backgammon."

At Simon's elbow, Arabella sat looking thoughtful, and occasionally swirling the drink around abstractedly in her glass. Bernadotti, black-garbed as usual, sat in a far corner plucking at his guitar. And as a background to the other sounds in the yacht's saloon, there was a regular *thwack* every seven or eight seconds as Pancho threw his knife repeatedly into the once polished surface of a coffee table a few feet from where he sat. For reasons best known to himself, he had changed out of his nonde-script clothes and was now sporting a light-coloured suit with a dark shirt and white

tie—an outfit in which, perhaps intention-
ally, he looked like the stereotype of a thir-
ties Chicago gangster.

Bernadotti abruptly stopped his strum-
ming, put the guitar aside, and spoke.

"Sun's almost gone down."

"Afraid of the dark, are we?" the Saint
enquired.

Descartes rolled the dice, regarded them
for an instant, and pounced triumphantly
back on the board with the piece that had
been removed.

"I regret, Monsieur *le Saint*, that we are
in something of a quandary regarding your
status on the—expedition. The vote of my
comrades is that upon darkness you shall go
overboard."

Bernadotti exposed his savage teeth in another wolfish grin, and repeated his earlier
throat-cutting gesture.

To Descartes, Simon said: "That would
be stupidly premature, for one simple
reason."

"And what is that?" asked Descartes, who
seemed willing to be convinced.

"Our Captain Finnegan is one man, usually drunk. Can any of you handle a vessel
this size, in possibly heavy weather?" He
looked from Descartes to Bernadotti to

Pancho. "None of you, I presume. Well, I can. So, it appears I'm going to be needed—as crew. At least for the time being."

Simon could see that the sense of his words had got through to Descartes, and he could also see the distrust in the eyes of the other two. Pancho made an unmistakable gesture towards the sea with his thumb. Bernadotti shook his head and spoke one word.

"Overboard."

Descartes regarded the Saint for a moment longer, and then made up his mind.

"Our Mister Saint, he is right. We have need of him—for the present. The fish can feast upon him when he is to us no longer useful."

Bernadotti hissed impatiently: "Let the fish have him now."

Descartes flushed with anger and he stabbed a pudgy forefinger in Bernadotti's direction.

"This is not a voting democracy! Silence, Enrico!"

"Good thought," said the Saint approvingly: at which Bernadotti came close, gripped his shoulder, and spoke through clenched teeth.

"Just watch your tongue, Templar. You

might still have an accident and fall over the rail."

Simon addressed himself to Descartes.

"I suggest you tell this goon to remove his greasy fingers from my shoulders before I break his arm," he said simply; and Descartes inclined his head in a gesture that instructed the goon to comply.

Bernadotti went back to his guitar with a final murderous glare at the Saint, and Simon and Descartes played on. After a while Descartes sat back in his chair, linked his fingers comfortably across that huge paunch, and regarded his opponent through narrowed eyes.

"Monsieur Templar," he said slowly. "Please gratify my curiosity, since we are to have your company for an uncertain period. How did it happen that you arrived at the *haras* in such a providential manner, to rescue Madame Tatenor?" He inclined his head towards Arabella in a token bow as he mentioned her.

"That's easy," the Saint told him. "Her perfume is very distinctive, and I have an acutely well-developed sense of smell. I once owned a bloodhound, and from him I picked up some of the basic skills of—"

"Monsieur Templar!" Descartes cut in reprovingly. "I ask from a genuine interest. And I ask also *how did you know of Tranchier?* You spoke his name, and yet . . . and yet, that was not the name given at the time of the boat explosion. From where, I ask you, did you have the information of his name?"

"Well, let's see," Simon began. "There are at least two possible explanations for that. One is that I made enquiries, through contacts of my own, and got the background on the so-called 'Fournier', including his real name, as well as on the bullion robbery that he—and you three, and Karl Schwarzkopf—committed."

"And the other explanation?"

The Saint glanced at Arabella, who was listening with close attention.

"You do all know that there was a sixth man involved, working from the Moroccan side?"

Descartes gestured towards the oil portrait of Tatenor.

"Only Karl knew him."

Simon raised his glass, held it up before him towards the portrait as if offering a toast, and drank.

Descartes went very still.

"You? Were *you* the sixth man?"

"I only said there was another possible explanation. What do *you* think?"

Descartes reflected, twirling his drooping moustache.

"No," he said finally. "I do not think it is likely that you are the sixth man."

"But *I* do," Arabella put in. "That's how you knew all about the gold, the robbery, the names, Charles, everything. And why you found me. Why you *had* to find me." She looked straight at him, with a kind of desperate sadness in her eyes. "What are you going to do with *me*, Simon? Overboard, like these swine have in mind for you?"

Simon returned her level gaze; and there was a sadness in his too, at the realisation that somewhere he had mishandled Arabella badly enough to have lost her trust, at least for the moment.

"Just remember," he told her gently, "that it was you who looked me up on the island, not the other way round." He looked at his watch. "Now I think it's time I took a turn at the helm."

There was a moment of tension as Bernadotti began to get up to stop him, but Descartes wagged a finger at the Italian.

"No—let Mr Templar work for his passage. And Captain Finnegan shall join our little party here."

"Let me make a suggestion," said the Saint. "When you pump him cleverly for information he hasn't got"—he gestured towards the bar—"use the *rye* whiskey on him, will you? There's only a bit of the good Scotch left." He found Finnegan already part-way lubricated and keeping somewhat unhappy company with an empty hip-flask. After commiserating with him over his, and their, enforced temporary compliance with the Descartes party's takeover, Simon sent him down for a rest and a refill, and took over the helm.

For perhaps half an hour he surrendered his thoughts to the soothing balm of the sea, as he had often done before in the course of innumerable adventures that had taken him upon it and under it. The weather was still fine and clear; the rays of the sinking sun, slanting forward from the starboard side, gilded the bows of the *Phoenix* as she rose and fell rhythmically on the slight swell, and the wavelets sparkled with a golden sheen that stretched ahead to the horizon. Finnegan had set a south-easterly course once they had cleared the Marseille harbour, which meant they were headed for Corsica

. . . And so Simon's thoughts were brought back before long to the events of the immediate past and to how they might develop, or be induced to develop, in the immediate future.

Even at the risk of further confusing or alienating Arabella for a time, he had played up the sixth-man mystery for the sake of the advantage it might be presumed to buy him with Descartes and his cronies. The Saint sensed that the more he could keep them guessing about his precise role and interest in the affair, the more time he was likely to gain. So long as he had time in hand, he had a sublime confidence that his resourcefulness, added to that generous providence which had always come up with some twist of events in his favour when he had needed it most, would win through in the end. Therefore his strategy was to play for as much time as he could: to watch and wait.

For the moment, he couldn't be sure how much any of the other principals in the developing drama of the *Phoenix* and the gold of Charles Tatenor actually knew or surmised. Descartes had clearly done enough thinking in the last day or two to have come to the same conclusion as Simon himself— Corsica held the key. At any rate, Descartes had told Finnegan to set the same course he would have set for Simon and Arabella had their uninvited guests not turned up. The Saint didn't know exactly how much Finnegan himself knew about the real purpose of those regular fishing trips to Corsica.

"Always the same little bay," he said, without giving any sign of attaching to that consistency of destination the significance which Simon, and evidently Descartes as well, suspected it had.

The Saint had familiarised himself with the instruments and studied the chart that had been unrolled and spread out, which included Marseilles at the north-west corner. It covered one sector in a large-scale Mediterranean series, and bore the number 12. He pulled out the drawers of a massive ship's plan-chest nearby and found them full of rolled-up charts of the same series, numbered up to 22. Number 12, of course, was missing; but so was number 18.

Which was an interesting piece of corroborative evidence, if any was needed, that they were headed in the direction most likely to yield something of interest. For the missing chart 18, according to the small-scale over-all map on the bulkhead over the chart drawers, covered an area which included the extreme south-western extremity of Corsica.

For the best part of an hour and a half more the Saint stood at the helm of the *Phoenix*, almost automatically making the necessary small corrections of course, as the pink and yellow of the sunset faded and the sky and sea darkened towards night.

His cogitations were interrupted when the door was opened, hesitantly, and Arabella came somewhat sheepishly into the wheel-house.

"Simon," she began, in a small and conciliatory voice, "I'm sorry if I've jumped to the wrong conclusions . . . sorry if I'm wrong . . . I mean, sorry if I *was* wrong. But all this—being threatened, abducted, nearly gored to death by a bull . . . people looking for gold, people waving guns at me . . . It's right outside my experience."

Simon nodded, smiled, and put his hands on her shoulders to look directly into the eyes that matched the blue of his own.

"I know that," he said simply. "The fact is, you've stood up to it all magnificently. Perhaps I should have got around to saying this before now. Very few women, or men for that matter, would have come out of that bull-ring ordeal as creditably as you did." The Saint put a finger under her chin, and kissed her lightly—with understanding rather than passion. "The fact is," he added, "I've worked alone too long now to be in the habit of sharing *all* my thoughts or hypotheses."

She searched his features reflectively.

"Well, try sharing *some* of them," she suggested.

Simon grinned, having seen that coming.

"I'll try to be less mysterious," he agreed.

"Starting now?" Arabella persisted.

"Starting right now. Fire away."

"Right. What do you think really happened on Charles's boat. You said you thought there was another man on board."

"Somebody," he said slowly, "got ashore from that boat just before she hit the rocks and blew up. I found a scuba outfit buried near the beach, and *someone* out of the normal run of rail passengers, someone with a French accent and without luggage, caught a train to London from the local station. It may not be much to go on, but it looks as if Fournier, as we knew him, set up the explosion to make it *appear* that the two of them had died in the crash."

"What about the *two* bodies they found in the wreckage?"

"That can be explained," Simon said. "Remember one thing. There was no positive identification of the bodies. Fournier could have hidden another body aboard before the race. Most likely an already dead body."

Arabella nodded keenly and thoughtfully.

"I see. And then, Tranchier would have knocked Charles out, jammed the helm at the right moment, and quietly vanished underwater, coming up on the beach while all eyes were on the blazing boat."

"You have to admit," said the Saint, "it sounds possible—in fact it sounds likely. Maybe Tranchier had got what he needed from Charles, namely the low-down on the gold and how to get it. And maybe he then got greedy. He had a bright idea. *He* would do a Charles, and keep all the remaining gold for himself. But to do that, and be able to enjoy it without constantly looking over his shoulder for Descartes and the others, he needed to convince *them,* as well as the rest of the world, that both he and Charles were no more."

Simon paused to turn on a chart-light in the wheel-house.

"What doesn't seem to have occurred to him," he continued, "was that Descartes

would be harder to shake off than that—
that he'd turn his attentions to you, as the
only other person who might have access to
the gold—assuming, of course, that there's
some left and that it *is* still in the form of
gold."

Arabella toyed thoughtfully with one of
the charts in the open drawer.

"And what do you think about that? *Is*
there gold? Is it in Corsica?"

"In Corsica?" He shook his head. "No. I
think there's gold all right, but I think it's
off Corsica. Somewhere in the sea. And I
think your Charles used to go back to that
spot in this yacht twice a year for the ex-
press purpose of bringing up a bar or two to
boost his bank balance—until the next
time."

Arabella pursed her lips in a long whistle
of amazed appreciation.

"Why, that's—that's perfect. What a
smart man he was! A secure private bank.
Just bring the gold up a bit at a time, sell it
discreetly someplace . . ."

Simon nodded agreement.

"The odd bar or two wouldn't attract too
much attention."

"The only weakness," she observed
thoughtfully, "—the one point of vulnera-

bility in his banking system—would appear to be Finnegan. Surely he must know about the gold?"

"Maybe," the Saint said. "The good Captain's still a bit of a question mark in my mind for the moment. But he certainly wasn't near enough to have toppled that crate; nor was *he* driving the van; nor did *he* stab Lebec's man in the Bidou Club. But somebody did."

"Then who?" No sooner had she spoken the words than she answered her own question. "You mean Fournier!" Then she added: "And where does the Saint's clairvoyance tell him Fournier is now?"

By way of a reply, Simon stepped outside on to the deck and pointed aft.

"See that speck on the horizon? It's a smallish boat, some kind of power cruiser. It's been following about ten miles behind us for at least the last couple of hours. I'd be willing to bet it's been on our tail ever since we left Marseille. And if it isn't Fournier," said the Saint, looking hard at Arabella as he paused, "I'd lay ten to one it's your friend Inspector Lebec."

——2————————————————

Jacques Descartes surveyed the limp piece of bacon on his fork as if mesmerised by it.

"It is a great institution, your English bacon and eggs, is it not?" he observed, entirely without conviction. "A breakfast which is yet adaptable for any mealtime."

"That's the best I could do," Arabella said, sulkily defensive, "with what I found on board. And anyway, I don't recall being hired as a cook—on my own yacht. You're lucky to get anything at all."

"Of course, Madame, of course," Descartes said hurriedly. "I did not mean . . . it is an excellent repast—an excellent impromptu repast."

He looked expectantly around the table, and after a slight delay some grudging grunts of assent were forthcoming from Bernadotti and Pancho.

Simon Templar, who had helped rinse the strips of bacon and spread them out to dry on a towel in the galley, after they had fallen into some washing-up water, thought it politic to change the subject.

"You were saying something to Mrs

Tatenor," he reminded Descartes. "About the bullion robbery."

"Ah yes—yes."

Descartes impaled another piece of bacon on his fork, dipped it into the congealing eggs on his plate, and conveyed it to his mouth with a valiantly repressed shudder. After minimal mastication he swallowed it with evident relief and made a visible effort to recover the mood of story-telling flamboyance which Arabella's culinary offerings had interrupted.

"Picture if you will, Madame—a crystal clear night. The moon is a brilliant yellow *cavaillon* melon . . . Suddenly—*there* is the ship. Outwardly a small passenger vessel, but in secret also a bullion ship. So low she floats in the water—so heavy with gold! Then—a burst of shots in the air, we stop her, we climb aboard. Everyone—hands up! We open the cargo hold—and there—there it is, gleaming in the moonlight. Gold, Madame—so much gold! Gleaming bricks of gold. So many, one could build a house from them!"

Descartes glanced at the faces of his audience of four—two of whom were remembering the night with him as he spoke. He continued with rising animation.

"So much gold! And all is perfect. No violence, as it was with the pirates of old. We had done it better—the shots only for effect. And then . . . ."

"Then—the champagne!" reminisced Bernadotti, his fork in his left hand and his automatic in his right where it had remained all through the evening.

"Yes!" Descartes beamed as he relived the excitement. "Some passengers are drinking champagne. We take it. We drink our own toast—to success!"

The Saint pushed his empty plate aside.

"And where's friend Karl during all this revelry?" he asked.

"Karl? He is in our boat. At the wheel, waiting." As he continued the story Descartes' smile slowly faded. "You will understand—Karl was employed with the Paris bank, and so he was important to the planning of the robbery. But also, even then, he was a driver of fast boats."

Arabella shifted impatiently on her chair.

"Well—what happened next?"

"The champagne, alas, was our undoing. We finished first the loading—we transfer the gold. Now our launch—*she* is low in the water, but still a very fast boat. We drink a final toast. Then suddenly, comes the

French coastguard—an armed boat! And we are caught."

He paused and leaned forward, his smile completely gone now, and his face reddening.

"Do you listen, Madame? We are caught —*except* for Karl, *and* the gold. *Brrrmmm!* He goes. Very fast. The gunboat shoots, he drives dodging. They chase—many miles. So it is told at the trial, *our* trial. But Karl— he escapes. And afterwards, there is prison for us."

"*We* get eight lousy years apiece in jail." Bernadotti spat the words out sourly. "And *your* goddamn Charles gets clean away. Pfft! Vanishes into thin air."

"Until last month," Descartes continued, "when we see a magazine regarding the boating, and the race which is to take place from the island. And there on the page—a photograph. He is older, yes. White hair, yes. A different name. But the same man. *Our* Karl Schwarzkopf!" He turned again to Arabella. "Madame, would you not, in our place, desire that gold?"

"Yes," said Arabella. "And in *my* place, too . . . Anyone for more bacon?"

During the answering rush of unenthusiasm Simon thought over the account they had just heard. It had certainly put some colourful flesh on what until then had been the bare bones of a story; but it had added nothing much of new substance, except perhaps the fact that Schwarzkopf, as he then was, had given the coastguard the slip after "many miles" in a good boat that must have been heavily weighed down with gold. Whether it could have reached the Coriscan coast from the vicinity of Marseille in one hop, or at all, was certainly open to question.

The *Phoenix*, however, had indubitably made that trip on a number of occasions, if Finnegan was to be believed; and she was now, as the night wore on, a good halfway there once again. A little while before, Simon had given the helm back, somewhat dubiously, to a Finnegan who was at least two sheets to the wind.

"Don't you worry. I could navigate her in me sleep, so I could," he had maintained.

Simon hoped it wouldn't come to that, but as a precaution he had insisted that Bernadotti receive some elementary instruction and be prepared to stand by as a reserve helmsman. This arranged, Simon and Arabella had at last settled their suitcases in the *Phoenix's* two comfortable guest staterooms. Descartes and his henchmen having cautiously elected to remain for the night in the saloon, that left Finnegan in continued occupation of his regular port-side cabin, which adjoined the galley.

Arabella, pleading tiredness, had gone to her cabin soon after the bacon-and-egg meal; and the Saint now decided to amble back up to the wheelhouse to reassess the current juggedness of Finnegan.

The two sheets to the wind had become two and a half, as the Saint had guessed from the movement of the boat. The bibulous Captain was groggy and bleary-eyed, but still standing.

"In Dublin's fair ci—ty," he sang, and wound the wheel right ". . .where the girls are so pret—ty, . . . I forrst set me eye—ees . . ." He wound the wheel left, as he sang unsteadily on: ". . . on sweet Mol—ly Ma— lone . . ."

Simon shook his head sadly in a kind of tolerant wonderment, and went aft to look out over the stern.

On the calm sea the *Phoenix*'s wake was clearly visible in the moonlight for perhaps half a mile back. It described a pronounced zig-zag; a small redeeming feature being that the directional trend of the wake, if the zig-zags were averaged out, was fairly consistent, which meant that Finnegan was at least managing to maintain the *Phoenix*'s over-all course.

The Saint was making his way forward again—having decided to leave Finnegan where he was for a while longer but to remove all and any further alcoholic temptation that might be at hand—when he became aware of a pulsating quality in the light reflecting off the sea on the ship's starboard side. At the same instant a bellow from Bernadotti, who happened to be on deck at the time, indicated that he too had noticed the pulsations of light and had likewise worked out what must be happening.

In her locked cabin, Arabella had removed the shade from a portable reading-lamp and stuck the bulb out of the porthole; and she was busily flashing an approximation of the Morse SOS signal into the night.

Bernadotti, still gripping his automatic, reached the cabin door within fifteen seconds, with the Saint just behind him. Bernadotti hammered on the door.

"C'mon, lady, turn that goddamn light out and open this door!"

It was clear that she had no intention of opening the door and every intention of continuing her signalling. It was as clear to Descartes, who appeared at the Saint's elbow with Pancho only moments later, as to Simon himself; and he turned at once to the deaf-mute and barked out an order, with exaggerated lip-movements to be sure of being understood at once.

"The fuses—quick! The engine room!"

If the Saint's opinion had been asked he would have had to agree that emergency action was called for. From Simon Templar's point of view, which was concerned with leaving himself plenty of room to manoeuvre without the complication of further intervention from outside, Arabella's distress-signal had to be stopped, and quickly. Already, as Pancho shot off down the companionway to the engine room, it might be too late. It would depend on the alertness of whoever was at the helm of the boat that had been keeping pace behind them. And it would depend, too, on who that was . . .

The lights went out suddenly; then, after a few seconds of total darkness, the corridor lights came back on. Pancho must have found the fuse or main switch for the cabin lights, for they could see that there was now only darkness where a strip of flashing light had previously been visible under the door of Arabella's cabin.

Descartes banged on the door.

"Open now!" he boomed. "Open, I say— or Enrico will shoot the lock. I will count to three only. One . . . Two . . ."

Bernadotti raised his automatic and Descartes stood aside.

"Three!"

The gun made a deafening crash that echoed and reverberated back and forth through the ship. The shot made a mess of the door and the jamb, but the lock itself still held— thus giving the lie to the countless western films in which lock-shooting is invariably and instantly successful.

Bernadotti charged the door with his shoulder, and the weakened jamb gave way. He dived into the cabin, grabbed Arabella roughly, and wrenched the lamp away from her. He gripped her painfully by the wrists and tried to drag her out; but she dug in her heels and fought back furiously with a hard kick to his shins followed by a strategically directed knee which caused him to double over in agony. When he finally straightened up it was with an extended string of Italian profanities; and then he advanced on Arabella with one fist upraised.

The Saint had followed him into the small and now unlighted cabin, and his first action was a preventive or, it might be termed, defensive one. The automatic was a nuisance and, so long as it remained in Bernadotti's grip, a dangerous nuisance. It took the Saint about four seconds to dispose of that hazard in a controlled manner. First the fingers of his left hand closed in a steely grip around the Italian's right lower wrist, effectively immobilising the joint to prevent the automatic from being turned and fired; and then one bony projecting knuckle of the Saint's other hand was jabbed up hard into the same wrist, where it found a pressure-point near the pulse. The effect was that Bernadotti's fingers sprang open as if by magic. The rest of Bernadotti yelped; and the gun, which was the object of the exercise, dropped to the cabin door. The Saint kicked it under the lower bunk, and proceeded from the defensive to the offensive phase of the operation.

He kept, and tightened, his grip on Bernadotti's right wrist; and then he moved in close and bent the arm hard up behind the Italian's back, bringing it to within an inch of the position that would break it or dislocate the shoulder.

And then, maintaining that grip, the Saint marched Bernadotti round to the door of the cabin, and with his other hand repeatedly banged the Italian's head against the doorframe.

"I know you prefer to fight women, Enrico," he said calmly during these exertions, "but don't ever do it again while I'm in the audience. Next time I *will* break your arm."

He released the arm and shoved Bernadotti away hard, so that he crashed into the bulkhead opposite the cabin door. But Simon had underestimated his resilience, and was caught partly off his guard by the sudden ferocity with which Bernadotti sprang back at him in a cursing rage for revenge. He succeeded in catching Simon with a hard but glancing blow to the side of the head, and for a few seconds a kaleidoscope of coloured lights danced before the Saint's eyes. Bernadotti had meanwhile sprang back to gather himself for a new rush. Simon waited, poised easily on the balls of his feet like the superbly fit fighting animal he was.

Arabella watched from inside the cabin; Descartes had quietly drawn an automatic of his own from a pocket, but he was making no attempt to influence the fight. And so Bernadotti hurled himself forward again, with wolf-teeth bared in a blood-lust of fury; and Simon Templar stepped aside adroitly and delivered a single hard forehand chop to the man's ribs.

There was a *whmmph* sound, and he fell back winded and gasping. Simon half-crouched, waiting for another rush . . .

But then something quite unexpected happened. Suddenly the corridor lights dimmed, almost to darkness; then, after a second or two, they brightened again, then dimmed . . . then brightened. And in time with those weird fluctuations of light there came from the direction of the engine room an even weirder sound, an unearthly laboured whining that climbed up and down the scale of musical pitch in synchronisation with the alternations of brighter and dimmer lighting.

"Pancho!"

Descartes' exclamation reminded them of what had been forgotten in the heat of the struggle: that the deaf-mute had not returned from his electrical mission in the engine room.

Descartes motioned urgently to Bernadotti, who limped off down the companion-

213

way to investigate after a final murderous glance at the Saint. Descartes flicked the barrel of his automatic to draw attention to it.

"Monsieur Templar," he said as the weird variations of light and sound continued. "You will please retrieve Enrico's weapon now, rather than later. *Carefully!* Holding the barrel! Thank you. Now give it to me." As Simon complied he added, "It was most careless of Enrico, was it not, to permit you to disarm him?"

It was then that the said Enrico reappeared grim-faced and shaken, and with naked fear in his eyes.

"Pancho is dead," he told them. "Strangled with his own tie—in the generator."

—3—

It was a scene of perfectly stark and graphically gruesome clarity.

There, heroically trying to keep on working, was the generator; and there lying across it was the prone and unquestionably dead body of Pancho Gomez, his tie caught in the flywheel spindle, which had dragged him in tight against itself. Sparks showered about his head with the periodic binding of the flywheel. The generator whined in varying pitch as it laboured against the unwonted resistance; and as its output fluctuated, so did the lighting.

All this could be, and was, taken in at a single glance. But to Simon Templar, and no doubt to the others, there was a central point of focus in that scene, a point that drew the attention inexorably and mesmerically, and made all the other details pale into mere backdrop. That compelling point of central and inescapable interest was the condition of the dead Pancho's face. It was blue; and from between the blubbery lips, now grotesquely parted, there protruded a hideously swollen purplish tongue. Pancho's ugliness in life had been remarkable, but it was nothing to his ugliness in death.

It was a sight which few can imagine who have not actually seen, as Simon Templar had seen a couple of times before, the victim of a strangulation. And even he found he needed to make a definite and deliberate effort to tear his eyes from the hypnotising sight of that lividly engorged tongue.

When he did tear himself from the sight,

215

he found he was the first to do so. The others were still standing frozen in horror-struck immobility when he reached forward to the mains box, took down the big battery lantern, and switched it on. He stopped the generator, and as the lights died he handed the lantern to Descartes to free both hands for the task of disengaging Pancho from the works. He managed it in a little while, with the sullen assistance of Bernadotti, and they lifted the body clear.

"Glory be!" said a familiar voice from behind, as they removed the last mangled pieces of the mauve tie.

And Finnegan appeared, clutching his hip-flask in the tight grip of a man who knows how to look after his possessions.

Simon blinked in astonishment.

"The helm, Captain!" he said. "What on earth are you doing down here?"

Finnegan made a smoothing-out gesture with his hands.

"Well, now, didn't I lash it tight? Sure it'll come to no harm for a minute or two." He moved forward to start up the generator again, shaking his head sadly. "And a nasty accident it was, to be sure."

"If it *was* an accident," Simon said slowly, looking hard at Finnegan.

"How what in the devil's name would he be doin' bendin' over the generator?" Finnegan puzzled aloud, either ignoring or not hearing Simon's comment.

As the lights came on, Descartes moved up close to him ominously, and Bernadotti did the same. Finnegan backed nervously away from them.

"Aw, you don't t'ink . . ." He eyed them disbelievingly as they fixed him with accusing glares. "How could I . . . ? How could it 'a had anyt'ing to do wit' me? Sure and didn't I just this minute pop down to see what the thrubble was? Wasn't I just in the wheelhouse—steering dhis ship for yous?"

"The ship is proceeding at this moment without your attentions at the helm," Descartes pointed out. "Why should we believe that you did not 'pop' here one minute earlier, and force the strangulation of our associate?"

Finnegan glared balefully from Descartes to Bernadotti and back to Descartes. Suddenly they grabbed one arm each and began to frog-march him away.

"I was in the wheelhouse, I tell yous!" Finnegan protested loudly as they got him up the companionway and out on deck.

Which was a considerable achievement in

view of the hindrance which Descartes' great quivering paunch represented to any serious physical endeavour relying on his contributory efforts. But somehow they managed it, with Simon and Arabella following closely behind. More than that, within seconds they had changed their grip on the hapless Finnegan—Bernadotti taking his feet and Descartes his hands—and had hoisted him bellowing on to the rail.

"Over he goes!" said Bernadotti.

"Stop!" the Saint called out with all the quiet authority he could muster; and it was just about enough. He spoke with the crisp urgency that the situation required. "Finnegan's the only one who can navigate us to that gold!"

Descartes and Bernadotti stood in frozen indecision for long moments. They could not be sure that Simon Templar was telling the truth; he might have already wormed the necessary details out of Finnegan himself. But it was not a point they could seriously afford to put to the test. Descartes spoke.

"As usual, Monsieur Templar, you are right. We must not be hasty . . ." They lowered Finnegan to the deck none too gently, and Descartes added, ". . . with the good Captain."

Finnegan, who in the last few minutes had sobered up probably faster than ever before in his life, tipped his cap to Simon and scuttled back towards the wheelhouse.

Descartes stood in silent thought for a minute or so, and then went determinedly after him. Simon followed, and so did Arabella; and Bernadotti tagged along too.

"Now!" they heard Descartes say, as the fat man completed the enterprise of squeezing his vast wobbling bulk up into the wheelhouse ahead of them. "It is time we had a truthful, a fully truthful conversation, my fine Captain Finnegan of the bottle!" He stood next to the helm with folded arms so that his presence would be impossible to ignore. "So—please begin the talking. Or we may yet change our minds and put you over the side!"

"I tell you, I had nothin' to do with it," Finnegan began.

"The gold! About the gold!"

Finnegan looked blank.

"Sure and didn't I tell yous before? Two or t'ree times. I know nothin' about any gold. What gold is it that you'd be t'inkin' of, now?"

"I am thinking of the gold that you and Mr Charles Tatenor would collect during your cruising to Corsica. So—to where on the island did you go?"

Finnegan eyed him warily, as he might have eyed a mad dog.

"We only went fishin', and that's the truth, so it is."

"And where exactly," Descartes demanded, looking searingly into Finnegan's face, "did you fish?"

Finnegan sighed with long-suffering patience.

"Like I said before—we'd anchor in a small bay. Always the same one."

"Why always the same bay?"

Finnegan shrugged.

"Mr Charles—he liked it there. And . . . he liked the next bay round. He'd go off around the headland in the dinghy—spearfishin'."

There was a long silence while the last revelation sank in. Descartes' eyes lighted up.

"So," he said softly. "We make progress at last."

"And you *are* taking us to that usual bay, aren't you?" Simon put in.

"Certain it is that I am," Finnegan said,

clearly relieved to have got off the hook so lightly after all. "And we'll be there in the mornin'."

Before they left him, Finnegan assured Simon that he was now revivified and daisy-fresh, and would happily stay at the helm through the night until they reached their destination.

"Not another drop," he told Simon earnestly, "shall pass these trut'ful ould lips this night."

Simon felt confident in the circumstances that the Captain would be as good as his word; and he was incidentally glad of the opportunity to get his own head down for a few hours of sleep in preparation for whatever tomorrow might bring.

"Time for some shuteye," he told Descartes as they left the wheelhouse.

"An excellent suggestion," Descartes agreed. He pointed with his automatic. "Down below—both of you. As you will have observed, Monsieur, *we* are now outnumbered, my one associate and I." He indicated Bernadotti. "And since the door to Madame's cabin cannot now be locked, you will both please to spend the night in the other cabin."

"You mean—together?" Arabella enquired frostily.

"I object strenuously," Simon protested, with evident delight.

"Now look here—" Arabella began; but Descartes' face and voice hardened.

"No, Madame! *You* look here," he told here. "And you do, please, as the weapon commands!"

And so it happened that Simon Templar came to be locked in a cabin with Arabella Tatenor; and it happened also that he awoke with the first light of dawn, as he had intended, and slid silently off his bed while she slumbered on in the one opposite.

Their luggage had been carefully searched, of course; but the Saint had one useful possession which nobody had thought worth confiscating; and that was a slim pencil flashlight. He put it in his pocket now in preparation for the early-morning walk which he intended to take as soon as he had disposed of the minor obstacle of the locked cabin door.

He examined the little heap of feminine impedimenta that Arabella had deposited on the dresser, and selected a promising-looking hairclip. The Saint's experience with locks and the techniques of opening them had been long and varied, and the cabin door would have delayed him only briefly in any case; but here he had an almost unfair advantage which made the enterprise childishly simple. He had been able to get a close-up view, not long before, of a similar lock on the damaged door of the next cabin, so that he knew exactly which type of mechanism he was dealing with.

Less than one minute later, after two minor adjustments to the bend he had made at the end of the clip, the lock gave a satisfying click as his makeshift instrument did the trick. Unfortunately that click also had a side-effect which he would have preferred it not to have.

It woke Arabella.

She rubbed her eyes and looked at him uncomprehendingly for a few moments where he knelt by the door.

"What are you doing?" she asked muzzily.

The Saint held up the bent clip and pointed to the door. Then he put his finger warningly to his lips. Arabella sat up and spoke in a firm whisper.

"OK. I'll keep quiet, but I'm coming along."

Simon shrugged his agreement to the ultimatum. He opened the door gradually, making scarcely a sound.

"Where to?" Arabella whispered.

"Finnegan's cabin. I want to see if he knows more than he's letting on."

They made their way noiselessly along the corridor and past the galley to Finnegan's cabin. But it yielded no surprises to the probing of the Saint's torch; it merely looked lived in, as indeed it had been. There was a bunk, with the bedding not very tidily straightened since it had last been used; there were a few books on a shelf, some magazines strewn about, and three or four empty bottles. The carpet had a grubby look, and some of Finnegan's clothes were hung untidily over a chair. It was, in short, just what might have been expected.

"Nothing untoward there," Simon had to concede as he closed the door again softly from the outside.

Arabella had glanced only briefly around the cabin with him, and now he found her by the open door of a small storage room that faced Finnegan's cabin.

"Look," she whispered. "Fishing gear."

The Saint looked. The store-room, lit by the pale dawn light slanting through a single porthole, was in a bit of a jumble, but he could see that besides the fishing gear various odds and ends were stacked there. There were some assorted cans of paint, a drum of paraffin, some hanks of cord and rope in various thicknesses, some lanterns and a couple of waterproof torches; there was a stack of folded rubber wet-suits—the Saint counted three—and the scuba outfits; a nylon mesh net; rods, reels, tackle boxes—and one large deep angler's basket complete with lid.

Simon picked up the basket curiously. It was sturdily constructed, and quite heavy. He took off the lid and peered inside. It was empty, but somehow the inside depth seemed less than the outside. He prodded the base from the inside, and it seemed to give slightly.

"Aha! Look here," he whispered. "Look at the base."

He tugged experimentally at the raffia weaving of the base. It moved—and then he found he could lift it up and out through the basket's top.

"A false bottom!" Arabella exclaimed. She reached inside, and pulled out a portable mariner's compass about six inches in diameter, and then a folded sheet of paper that had been hidden beneath the compass.

It was the missing nautical chart number eighteen.

"Well, well," Simon said quietly. "Here it is—the bay where the fishing, I'll warrant, may be the best in all Corsica."

Arabella squinted down at the chart.

"What are those pencil lines and whatnot?"

"Seventy-three degrees—white villa," the Saint read. "Three hundred and forty-eight degrees—lighthouse . . . They're bearings on shore landmarks, taken from the sea."

"So the point where they intersect . . ."

". . . must be where the gold is," Simon finished.

"Bravo!" boomed out the voice of Jacques Descartes from behind them. "Excellent work. I congratulate you both!"

—4—

By the middle of the morning the *Phoenix* lay anchor in a very small and very blue bay in the deeply indented south-west coast of Corsica, and Captain William Finnegan had gone to his bed clutching a newly replenished flask of his favourite spirituous comfort.

During breakfast, the Saint had contrived to come to what he regarded as satisfactory terms with Descartes over the next stage of their working relationship. In spite of the two automatics which now covered his movements more consistently than before, and which might have had an inhibiting effect on a less robust personality than Simon Templar's, he had been at his most relaxed and amiable. He had taken what pleasure he could in the breakfast itself; and when Arabella's attention was momentarily elsewhere he had occasionally winced in sympathy as he watched Descartes bravely swallowing his gastronomic scruples along with some tepid and lumpy porridge. The Saint had even made a point of finding the time and patience to play two more games of backgammon—and to make sure of narrowly losing. But most important, he had been able to argue convincingly enough that he was the only member of the party with any knowledge or experience of diving.

In truth, he had not had to argue very hard, even in the face of Bernadotti's simmering hatred. That somebody would have to go down under the water, to see what, if anything, was to be found in the place marked on Tatenor's hidden chart, was self-evident; and the Saint was the obvious if not the only possible choice.

And that, for the moment, was enough for Simon Templar. So long as he could extend his practical usefulness to Descartes, so long would he succeed in extending his own life. For he had not the slightest doubt that once the time of that usefulness was manifestly at an end, Descartes would kill him with no more compunction than he would have spared for a fly that had trespassed upon his *petit pain,* or a beetle as he ground it underfoot . . . And as things stood now, that time would come only after, not before, the burning question of the gold had finally been answered one way or another. As before, the Saint reasoned that so long as he had time he had a world of prospects for somehow, given a moderately friendly disposal of destinies, retrieving his and Arabella's—and Finnegan's—fortunes from under the shadow of Descartes' uncomfortable influence.

Nevertheless, nobody with the smallest knowledge of the Saint's character and history would doubt that he had been sorely tempted to improve his position by some spectacular and decisive action. If he had had no one but himself to consider, he would certainly have contrived an ambush, or some other plan, to secure one of the automatics for his own use and thereby level the odds. But he didn't have only himself to think of; and an ambush would have carried a degree of risk in which he preferred not to involve the others until there was no other choice.

Therefore it was the waiting game still; and it was against that background that Simon and Arabella prepared to set off in the *Phoenix*'s rubber dinghy.

When they had lowered the boat into the placid waters of the bay, Descartes got in clumsily, his ponderous bulk all but capsizing the boat. Simon and Arabella followed, watched by a surly and suspicious-looking Bernadotti at the rail.

"How can I know you're even gonna come back—if you do find the gold?" he demanded.

Descartes' deep chuckle floated across the water as they pushed the dinghy off.

"Dear Enrico! Be relaxed. This boat can scarcely contain even its present loading." He patted his stomach significantly. "It is far too small for much gold. We will have to come back for the yacht. Somebody has to remain here to keep observation on Finnegan."

The Saint had already put on his wet-suit and weightbelt. Now he yanked the T-cord to whip the outboard into puttering life, and pointed the stubby nose of the dinghy obliquely out to sea. For two hundred yards or so he took the dinghy out in almost exactly the direction from which the *Phoenix* had only recently arrived; and his keen eyesight did not fail to note that the tiny dark smudge was still on the horizon, and at the distance it had maintained since he had first spotted it early that morning while the *Phoenix* was still under way.

And if Jacques Descartes had been watching the Saint's features very closely, and had known how to read the signs on that lean tanned face, he might have seen, faintly and evanescently, the merest shadow of a ghostly smile playing at the corners of Simon's mouth as he took the dinghy up to speed and turned round the narrow verdant headland that formed the little bay's northern margin.

A few minutes later, with the headland behind them, he slacked the throttle right off and let the engine idle for a minute while he (quite literally) got his bearings.

They were in the next bay. Small and blue like the one they had just left, this was the bay where the pencil marks had been made on the chart—the bay, presumably, where Charles Tatenor had "spearfished" while the headland conveniently blocked Finnegan's view from the *Phoenix*. Simon checked with the compact but finely graduated compass they had found in the false-bottomed fishing basket, sighting on a white villa near the beach. Then he opened the throttle briefly to take the boat a few yards farther across the bay.

"Seventy-three degrees to the white villa," he announced. "Spot on." He turned his attention to the lighthouse on the next headland. "Three hundred and forty-eight we want, three hundred and fifty-six we've got. So we're a fraction too far out. If we head straight for the villa . . ."

A few minutes later he raised a thumb in the air to indicate success, and slung the anchor overboard.

"*Bon!*" said Descartes.

In his impatience and obvious excitement he peered at the sea on both sides of the dinghy as if he expected to see clearly through the wavelets and the forty feet of water to the sea bed beneath.

"Thanks—partner," said the Saint sardonically, as he put on his flippers.

Arabella helped strap the scuba tanks on his back, with their breathing-tubes and mouthpiece. He donned the face mask, sat on the side of the boat, put in the mouthpiece, and back-flipped into the sea.

It was some time since he had done any diving, but to him it was one of those physical activities that had a unique feel which the body never forgot; like swimming itself.

Here, according to the chart, the water was some six to seven fathoms deep—comfortably within the range of scuba equipment. Yet all diving, no matter how straightforward, brought with it something of the same eerie sense of otherworldly adventure. The wonder began with the first moment, when the water closed over his mask, and years fell away as if they had never been, as though he had made his last dive only the day before. In an instant he crossed from the ordinary and familiar world of light into that other and very different world, the ultimate dim green world of the undersea. All the eye-aching brightness above was replaced at once by a cool translucence of fluid jade. And with that came the ecstasy of weightlessness, the dream-like ability to move in three dimensions almost without effort.

With a few lazy kicks of his flippers, he sent himself gliding down towards the sea bed. At a depth of about fifteen feet, he stopped to look back at the sea's surface. It was like a vast ceiling of liquid glass, wrinkling and rolling in long undulations, with the underside of the dinghy projecting down through it and partaking in its rhythmical movement.

The Saint went down into the deepening green. A school of hundreds upon hundreds of tiny silver-and-yellow fish flicked noiselessly past him, and some of their bigger cousins peered pop-eyed through the glass of his mask as they followed him curiously down. Then a spur of jagged rock rose to meet him out of the olive twilight; some fronds of slimy weed brushed at his legs for a moment; and then he was within arm's length of the bottom.

He gazed around at the glaucous world of weeds and fishes. The sea bed was mostly sandy there, but it was far from flat, and there were little forests of marine growths at intervals for as far as his eyes could see in the soft gloom. He turned and surveyed the sea bed in the opposite direction. The same irregular landscape, if it can be called a landscape, met his probing eyes.

And then he saw it. It was perhaps twenty yards away, and it could only have been the remains of a boat.

At first glance he had taken it for another patch of the almost fluorescently tinted seaweed; but on longer inspection the shape of a largish cabin cruiser was unmistakable. Simon swam towards it, and as he came closer he could easily understand how he had almost been deceived on that first glance; for the sunken boat was almost overgrown by variegated algae. The Saint had, as a matter of fact, had a lucky line of sight, from which it was the sharp point of her bows that had caught his eyes. If he had been looking from any other angle, he might never have seen anything but the splodge of weed . . . And perhaps, he thought as he swam the last few yards towards the sunken hull, that was a good omen.

The first thing he noticed was the big jagged hole in her transom. He examined the hole closely for a moment; he had seen enough shellfire damage before to be sure that he was looking at an example of it now. This must be the boat in which Schwarzkopf-Tatenor had made his run for it; and therefore Simon Templar knew that he was surely approaching the moment when his theory—for it had little right to be called anything more—would be put to the final test. He was well aware of the many "ifs" and "buts" he had glossed over, perhaps too slickly, in the speculations which he had shared with Arabella the previous night in a corner of that bright blue world forty feet above him. He looked up again at the high liquid ceiling. It was dimmed from this depth, but he could still make out the underside of the dinghy, now well to the edge of his field of view.

Yes, he knew his hypothesis was just that, on any objective view. That Charles Tatenor had kept his gold eleven years ago, rather than finding some immediate way of turning it into cash; that he had continued to keep it during those years since; that he had paced his "spending" of his hoard so that a good proportion of the original amount might still remain; and finally that he had kept that hoard, not in a series of safe deposit boxes around the world, not buried in a cave on dry land, nor in any of a hundred other good and possible hiding places, but just exactly where it had sunk—in forty feet of water, in the locker of Davy Jones.

That was the postulate: and the Saint knew that at any step in the reasoning,

Charles Tatenor might not have acted in the way which that reasoning assumed. But the Saint's thinking was characterised by those occasional intuitive leaps of great boldness, which had usually proved justified when they had been trusted in the past. And that was why—supported now by the evidence of the chart and its annotations, which certainly suggested something of interest down there—he expected to find gold in the sunken cabin cruiser he had discovered in the silent depths of the sea.

Slowly he finned his way along the length of the boat and back along the other side, the silence broken only by the regular suck of his own breath drawn in from the compressed-air tanks on his back, and the gurgle of the escaping bubbles that trailed upwards as he exhaled. He saw weird and garish fish flitting at their leisure between the rusting railings that had long been in-corporated into their submarine world. He saw the slow sure accretions of eleven years, the barnacles and sea urchins which had colonised the superstructure. He saw the wheelhouse that was now an eerie undersea cave where a school of small translucent squid were pumping themselves sporadically along beneath the sodden and rotting remains of the helm. And he saw the big hatchway set in the after-deck, its fastenings still gleaming with a faint metallic sheen and still relatively free from the encroaching weeds . . . as if it had seen some use over the years.

He examined the hatchway cover. It looked massive, and the fastenings seemed to be of tarnished brass. They included a big solid pair of hinges, two spring latches, and a large heavy brass ring.

The Saint released the latches without difficulty. He grasped the ring and twisted it first one way and then the other. He felt the fastening mechanism yield reluctantly. He braced himself against the railings with his feet, and heaved up on the ring with both hands.

Slowly, against the treacle-like resistance of the water, the hatchway cover opened. The Saint let it come to rest on the deck in the open position, and then he unclipped the compact but powerful underwater torch from his weightbelt.

He switched it on and directed the beam into the open space below.

It was deep—perhaps six feet or so. And the bottom seemed to be completely filled with what looked like lumpy sand.

VI: How Bernadotti was Discovered, and the Phoenix was set loose.

—1—

Simon Templar swam head-first into the cabin below; and he would have been the first to admit that the hands with which he began to scrape at the sand had lost some of their accustomed steadiness.

Almost as soon as his fingers began to burrow, they came up against something more solid. He pushed some of the sand aside, and shone the light full on the area he had partially cleared.

And between the grains of sands he saw the fabulous glistening gleam of gold.

He scraped some more sand away; and almost in a dream he saw them. Brick upon brick, or bar upon bar—the terminology was the least important thing at that moment— they were piled up inside the sunken launch, under that mere sprinkling of sand.

And even though the Saint had been at least half expecting it, still the actual discovery of all that gold was a wonder and a marvel now that it lay there before him in tangible reality. Its permanent brightness had always been the prime attraction of that malleable yellow metal upon which the fates of nations had risen and fallen. Too soft to share many practical uses with humbler metals, it had become sought after not only for its rarity but also for that very chemical inertness which had preserved the hoard under his hands from the normally corrosive sea.

No naturally occurring substance will make so much as a chemical dent in gold: that is why, almost alone among metals, it is found in the free state as gleaming nuggets or dust of the pure element. Only *aqua regia*, a mixture of concentrated nitric and hydrochloric acids in the "royal" proportions, can attack it. And that is why gold has been so prized by almost every civilisation and pre-civilised society that ever was.

In every country where it has been found, people had made religious artefacts from it. They had fashioned art and jewellery of it; craftsmen had given their lives to working with it; armies had been raised for it, wars started for it and stopped for it. Loves were traditionally sealed with it; it was the bedrock of currencies and economies; generations of men and women had schemed and lied and cheated and stolen and killed for it.

And Simon Templar was looking at maybe eight million dollars' worth of it at current values.

It was not the first gold he had seen in bulk, and if the fates gave him half a chance it would not be the last. There had even been a time, years before, when he had gazed upon another underwater hoard of gold, and had played his part in bringing it to the surface, and finally in consigning its possessor to the deep in its place. But that was another adventure, one that had passed into memory with so much else; and this was a new sea, and there were new villains to do battle with, and a new heroine, and the gold of here and now.

He lifted one of the ingots to test its underwater weight, and then he let it fall back.

It was not easy to heave a deep sigh from within the respiratory encumbrances of a scuba-diving mask, mouthpiece and other paraphernalia. But the Saint, who could do many things that were not easy, managed to heave one, in spirit at least. The sigh that he heaved was profoundly heartfelt, the sigh of a man deliciously tantalised, a sigh of high aspiration and rich romantic yearning. To be confronted with such a splendiferous superabundance of boodle, which moreover must have been long given up for lost by its rightful owners, and to have no immediately available means of appropriating it for his own use, was almost more than a red-blooded freelance buccaneer could bear. Even such a seasoned practitioner of freebooting as himself, with all his experience of mouthwatering loot in every conceivable form and denomination, could hardly be blasé about such a prodigious heap of solid swag as that.

His mind reviewed the situation objectively, once again, as he shifted a few of the ingots to check his estimate of their depth in the cargo hold, and their number.

Up above, Descartes would be waiting— waiting and wondering, with the automatic on his knee and Arabella beside him. Obviously the Saint had to go back to the dinghy, and just as obviously his prudent policy of saving their skins for as long as possible would dictate that he tell Descartes about the gold, even if not all about it . . .

He spent only a short while longer inside the boat; then, leaving the hatch open, he glided back and upwards through the lightening green, to break surface beside the dinghy.

As he climbed aboard, blinking at the glare of the sun and pushing back his facemask, Descartes leaned forward eagerly, with the automatic held loosely in his hand.

"Anything?"

Simon slipped out of the tanks, and took off his flippers expressionlessly.

"Well?" Arabella insisted.

Simon towelled calmly, as if he had just returned from a purely recreational swim.

"Well?" Descartes demanded. "Is it down there?"

In reply the Saint picked up an orange marker-buoy and dropped it overboard, throwing its anchor after it.

Descartes' eyes widened with delighted realisation.

"Yes? Is it really there? The gold is there?"

"I'd say a good four, maybe five million dollars' worth." The Saint halved his own estimate with a straight face. "It's certainly going to mean a fortune for somebody."

"*Magnifique!*"

Simon looked steadily at him.

"We're in luck, aren't we, *partner*."

Descartes hesitated; and then a broad and

242

cunning smile, rich with gold of its own, spread across his face.

"Well done—partner," he agreed.

The Saint was under no illusions about that, of course. He was quite sure that Descartes was going along with the implications of partnership for one reason only, which was a simple and practical one. The gold was still at the bottom of the sea, and the physical task of bringing it up remained. Whatever system they might manage to rig for getting it aboard, a diver would be needed. It might take a dozen dives or more; but somebody would have to go down there. And that somebody was certainly not going to be Jacques Descartes.

And once again, it suited the Saint to be useful.

He stood up and stretched.

"Well," he said, "why don't we go and fetch the *Phoenix*—and get to work?"

There was no dissent to that suggestion; and as he started up the dinghy and turned it around to head back the way they had come, he told them briefly about the sunken boat.

"One of those coastguard shells must have hit it," he said. "The boat must have been

243

sinking as he came around the headland here."

"The luck of the man!" Descartes exclaimed. "He could have done it no better if he had planned it. To finish with such a *cache* which only he could find again!"

The Saint nodded.

"It was perfect. And the gold he left there was even earning a dividend, in a way."

"A dividend? How do you mean?" Arabella's brow creased.

"The value of gold fluctuates," Simon said. "But it's usually risen in the long run, and by more than the cost of living. So in real terms the gold he kept was an appreciating asset, year by year."

Descartes leaned over with narrowed eyes, and tugged reflectively at his moustache.

"Then how does it happen, Monsieur Templar," he said with a slow intentness of curiosity, "that the gold was worth five million dollars eleven years ago, and is now, according to your estimate, worth less?"

"That's easy," said the Saint, without batting an eyelid. "Our Karl was spending it. Maybe he was greedy. Or maybe he took a risk in the beginning, and cashed a big slice of it in, right away. Maybe he's got a few million stashed away in numbered Swiss

244

bank accounts that we'll never know about. Maybe he did keep it all as gold, but moved some elsewhere. Maybe he was nervous about keeping all his golden eggs in one basket. Maybe—"

The Saint's glibly assured string of "maybes" stopped in mid-air, not because his fertile brain had run out of postulated reasons why the quality of gold eventually brought up might be less by a hefty margin than Descartes might like, but because, as they approached the headland, they had just caught sight of the *Phoenix* coming around it towards them.

"Enrico, the fool! What is that suspicious idiot doing?" Descartes shouted.

He glared, jumped up off-centre in the dinghy, and again very nearly capsized it. For a moment he teetered comically, and then he sat heavily down.

The *Phoenix* was perhaps three or four hundred yards away and making good speed as she came towards them. Descartes had gone as red as the proverbial lobster at the thought that Bernadotti had taken it upon himself to bring the *Phoenix* around the point ahead of time, or had had Finnegan do it, in defiance of his instructions; but to Simon it seemed a fairly unimportant piece of self-assertion. Within seconds, he had adjusted his mind to the minor change of plan, and it was in that adaptive frame of mind that he throttled back the engine of the dinghy and began a leisurely turn to retrace their tracks towards the orange marker, which was presumably the yacht's destination also, now that it was within sight. As he did so, he let his mind dwell on the practical task ahead. He had already assessed the number of gold bars—weighing exactly one kilogram each on dry land—that lay down there in the cargo hold under the sea; and now he occupied himself for a few seconds with some mental arithmetic.

There had been many moments in his adventure-crammed life when he had smelt danger ahead of time—when some seventh sense had tipped him off while there was yet a tissue-thin margin of milliseconds remaining—before the ground fell away as a sheer cliff-edge, or the bomb burst, or someone squeezed a trigger behind him or opened a trap-door to oblivion in front of him. But there were also times when, since he was human too, that early-warning system simply failed to operate—or operated only in the very last scintilla of time, when there was no space for considered action or decision, but only the autonomic "flight or fight" reaction of instinct to a threat too sudden to allow the intervention of anything as slow as thought.

And it was something like that for Simon Templar now, as his mind busied itself with thoughts of the gold bars awaiting collection, and of the means to be employed for that collection and of the number of dives he might have to make . . . while the *Phoenix* turned slightly so as to continue bearing down directly on the small rubber dinghy.

He had her in his field of vision the whole time, but his full attention was aroused only when Descartes and Arabella let out strangled yells at the same moment; and then the bows of the *Phoenix* were almost upon them.

Before he realised what he had done, Simon had grabbed Arabella's hand and yanked her over the side with him in a double dive that took them some five feet under.

They surfaced, with Arabella spluttering and coughing from the water she had inhaled, and looked around. The *Phoenix* had tossed the little dinghy aside like a cork, and they could see it still bobbing about, now upside down on the sea, but holed and sinking fast, as the yacht continued on her course. But of Descartes there was no sign.

Simon duck-dived as the stern of the *Phoenix* passed them, perhaps twenty feet away. And under the waves he saw the great gross form of Jacques Descartes being drawn inexorably into the churning propellers.

There was absolutely nothing that anyone could have done at this point. Simon surfaced again and waited for Descartes' body to appear, which it did after a few seconds, with a blood-red stain spreading around it, as the *Phoenix* ploughed on away from them.

—2—

Whatever else this new and totally unforseen development might mean, for the Saint and Arabella it certainly meant that their business with Jacques Descartes had been concluded in the most dramatic and final way possible. But it was by no means clear to either of them that their new situation represented an improvement over the uneasy bond of necessity which they—or at any rate Simon on behalf of them both—had had with the not totally dislikeable Frenchman whose gross and mangled body now floated belly-down on the surface of the sea.

Whoever was at the helm of the *Phoenix* had inexorably staked his own claim to the gold, and had demonstrated at the same time, with the chilling clarity of ice, his attitude to any competing claims. He had simply and efficiently mown the three of them down; and that he had not bothered to stop to see whether they were alive or dead was evidence of a singlemindedness which made even Simon Templar catch his breath.

It had not escaped him, however, that he was lucky to have breath to catch, after having allowed himself to be caught so thoroughly off his guard by the *Phoenix* on her deliberate collision course. And it had not escaped either him or Arabella that on an immediate practical level the options now open to them were starkly limited. Either they could stay where they were, treading water until they eventually drowned, or they could start swimming for the shore.

They started swimming.

But they had swum no more than a hundred yards when they heard the drumming of another boat's engines behind them. They turned, and waved and splashed and shouted, but clearly they had already been seen.

The boat was a motor launch bearing the markings of the French coastguard; and as it came towards them they recognised the slightly pudgy form of Inspector Gérard Lebec.

"Thanks," Simon said as they were helped aboard. "Small world, isn't it?"

Lebec's pale green eyes looked expressionlessly at the Saint. He nodded, then barked an order in French to the man at the helm. The man gunned the motor briefly and took the launch around in a tight turn to where the body of Descartes floated on the waves.

After Simon had helped him to fish the body out of the sea and lift it aboard, Lebec said: "So—you receive police hospitality once more, Monsieur Templar."

"I'll admit, I never thought I'd be glad to see *you*, Inspector," the Saint said easily. "Very lucky, the way you just happened along like that."

"I have been following behind you since Marseille," Lebec said shortly, and turned to Arabella. "It was very wise of you, Madame, to telephone me before your departure."

That was no real surprise to Simon. He had suspected something of the sort as a possibility after he had first observed that they had company; and he had regarded Arabella's brief foray into private-enterprise distress signalling as more or less clinching evidence.

He cocked a quizzical and challenging eye at her. For a while she tried rather awkwardly and shamefacedly to avoid his direct gaze, but he was remorseless in searching out her eyes; and finally she turned and looked at him defiantly.

"Well—it *is* lucky he was here to pick us up out of the sea," she said. "And all I did was follow police instructions by reporting that we were leaving Marseilles."

The Saint nodded, his thoughts working to accommodate all the new factors that had suddenly entered the picture. Descartes had gone, abruptly; and just as abruptly, Lebec had appeared. And there was now the mystery of the *Phoenix*, and of who had been at the helm a few minutes ago. But whatever the changes in principal actors, there was one central focus of interest in that picture, and that was what Simon hung on to. Just across the water was a fabulous hoard of gold, lying only forty feet down; and he wanted a good proportion of it to finish up in his own personal coffers.

"Inspector Lebec," he said pleasantly. "Would you like me to tell you where there's four million dollars' worth of gold bars?"

Lebec gestured towards the now stationary *Phoenix*.

"I think I can guess that, Monsieur Templar."

The *Phoenix* lay at anchor, her engines stopped. She was still, silent, and devoid of any sign of life. They had taken a wide circular line in the launch, and approached from her bows, not knowing quite what they might find. The wheelhouse, and the decks, were apparently deserted. At a signal from Lebec the helmsman brought the launch close in alongside.

"There may be some trouble, Madame," Lebec said. "You will please remain here." He turned to the Saint. "And you—you will accompany me, Monsieur Templar."

Simon followed Lebec, making something between a long pace and a short jump from the roof of the launch's cabin to the deck of the *Phoenix*.

The Saint could have recalled many occasions in his life when tension-filled minutes had seemed to drag into interminable hours.

Those were the times when he had been most vulnerable, for one reason or another, and the enemy had been at his most inscrutably and dangerously unpredictable. But of all that array of nerve-stretchingly unenjoyable situations, there were few in which he had felt so helplessly, fleshcrawlingly exposed, so wide open to the whim or mercy of someone unknown, as he did now, prowling watchfully around the *Phoenix*'s decks and accommodation. Lebec was at least armed. The Saint wasn't; and the comfort that he was able to draw from the presence of an automatic in the detective's hand was realistically limited compared with the comfort it would have given him to have one in his own . . . Over and above which, he had reasons enough, from his point of view, for feeling uncomfortable about any degree of personal dependence on Lebec.

Lebec led the way cautiously into the saloon. There was no one there. The wheelhouse, likewise, was deserted. So were the staterooms the Saint and Arabella had used. And so was the Captain's cabin. There was no sign of anybody on board.

"It seems that we have on our hands a ghost ship," Lebec said.

And then, right on cue as it seemed, they

heard a sound which caused the hairs on the back of Simon Templar's neck to stand up as if in response to the caress of an icy feather.

It was a weird strangled gurgling sound, a plangent wail with all the evil-laden menace of an unseen tomcat sending its persistent yowling threats into the night.

They stood still and listened, Lebec with his automatic poised.

And then the note of the caterwauling changed, and Simon heard in that sound a timbre, a quality of deeper resonance, which he knew he had heard somewhere before. He listened again, with his head on one side. It seemed to be coming from not far away. And as he listened he began to hear some distinguishable component noises, almost like syllables, in that dreadful blood-curdling wailing. It began to sound, so it seemed to him, something like "Toorooroo-roro—loorarroo . . ."

Then suddenly it came to him; and with his heart dropping through his stomach with helpless dizzy laughter and relief, he turned the key in the locked door of the storeroom, the only place where they had not looked, and opened the door to reveal, prone among the paint cans and paraffin, one standard pie-eyed Finnegan, complete with bottle.

Finnegan sang.

> . . . *loo-ra loo-ra,*
> Dhat's an Oi-i-rish lo-lla . . ."

He broke off, squinting vaguely at the Saint and Lebec. Then his eyes rolled happily.

"Good afternoon, Captain," said the Saint kindly. "No point in asking how you are. We can see you're very well. But, Captain—somebody locked you in here. Did you see who? Was it Bernadotti?"

He might as well have put the question in Serbo-Croat to a deaf Chinese hedgehog. Finnegan snored blissfully.

Simon and Lebec carried him to his cabin, laid him on his bunk, and went back on deck.

"What now?" asked the Saint. "He didn't lock *himself* in there, that's for sure."

Lebec stroked his chin thoughtfully for a moment.

"The gold must be recovered. You, as its finder, will qualify for the reward offered by the Government of France. I will support your claim, Monsieur Templar. But I require your services as diver."

Simon could not have hoped for a better opening.

"Agreed," he said. "Ten percent?"

The Saint had made a preliminary shallow dive to guide Lebec in bringing the *Phoenix* as near as possible directly over the sunken hoard, and he was ready to go down and load up for the first time. He had remembered the tough nylon net he had seen in the store room, and had tied it to a strong length of rope in such a way that it could be made secure after loading, so that Lebec, using the spare winch, could bring the loaded net up without risk of spilling any of its contents.

By the Saint's estimate there were possibly six or seven hundred of the gold ingots to be brought up. That made six or seven hundred kilograms, or getting on for three-quarters of a ton of gold to be retrieved, using a net intended for fishing. There was no point in taking a risk of overloading the net, and Simon judged that sixty bars would be the most they could safely try to bring up in a single load. That meant he would have ten or twelve dives to make.

While he was getting all that exercise, there would be plenty to occupy his mind. As he began to take the net down for the first time, he found himself coming back again to a fantastically improbable notion which he hadn't yet found a way of entirely dismissing from his thoughts.

It was the notion that Finnegan might not be all that he seemed; that his drunkenness was a pretence and a blind, merely the product of brilliantly convincing acting; that the seemingly innocent Irishman *had* after all done all those things of which the Saint had previously judged him incapable.

Simon swam down into the sunken cruiser, spread out the net on top of the golden hoard, and began loading it for the first time, with his mind still following that same corridor of thought—or was it a blind alley? Could Finnegan have been the shadowy man in the Bidou Club after all? Had he escaped in the blue van, only to reappear a few minutes later, stumbling about and carolling squiffily? Could Finnegan have "forced the strangulation" of Pancho, as Descartes had put it? And had Finnegan been the man at the helm, perhaps even humming a little ditty, when the *Phoenix* rammed the dinghy?

He had to admit to himself that it was just about possible. Finnegan *could* have done all these things. But had he? If he had, it was an acting achievement to stagger the imagination, a *tour de force* rivalling or surpassing the best the Saint had ever seen—and the Saint had seen some.

And again, if Finnegan had done all those things, there was still the toppling crate to be explained. There was still no way, as far as Simon could see, that the Irishman could have been responsible for that. Of course, it could conceivably have been a genuine accident; but wasn't that stretching the theory too far—piling coincidence on top of fantasy?

And then there was the question of how Finnegan could have managed that last mind-boggling feat of locking himself in the store-room and leaving the key on the outside of the door.

The Saint's mind continued to work at the problem as he steadily transferred the first clutch of gold to the net. Perhaps Bernadotti had locked Finnegan in? Perhaps he had realised what Finnegan was really up to, and had put him away to immobilise him while . . . While what? And in that case, where had Bernadotti vanished to?

That question was the one that continued to echo most persistently through his thoughts.

In any case, where was Bernadotti?

But to pile puzzle upon puzzle, there was another missing party—one who, on an earlier hypothesis, would have been expected to show up before now. And that was Tranchier.

The idea that Tranchier was still alive and anxious to grab all the swag for himself had once seemed reasonable enough, but now the Saint was no longer so sure. If Tranchier was alive and knew that the *Phoenix* held the secret of the gold, why hadn't the fish-faced Frenchman shown his phizzog?

Finnegan, Bernadotti, perhaps Tranchier, . . . two dead bodies . . . and the gold of Schwarzkopf-Tatenor. As Simon added the final few gold bars to complete the first load, he stepped off that carousel of thought and speculation and back on again, with the same question ringing in his head like a refrain.

Where was Bernadotti?

He tried a different tack, turning the reasoning around the other way. If Finnegan was as innocent as he appeared, why wasn't Bernadotti there on the *Phoenix?*

There seemed to be only two reasonable

explanations. The first was that Bernadotti was deliberately keeping himself hidden, and the second was that he had been got rid of.

The Saint couldn't put it to himself any more neatly than that. If it was the former, it was hard to see that Bernadotti would have had time to hide anywhere except on the ship; but he had not been found there, and Simon was confident that no hiding place had been overlooked. And if it was the latter—if somebody had got rid of Bernadotti—well, at least his body could have been dumped in the other bay . . . And then, things would look decidedly black for Finnegan.

With the first quota of bars loaded, Simon fastened the net securely at the top and tugged sharply on the rope to signal Lebec and his crewmen to start hauling. He steadied the net as it began to move; but the pull up was not quite vertical—perhaps the repositioning of the *Phoenix* above had been slightly out, or perhaps a tide was dragging the heavy load. At any rate, as soon as the loaded net had been pulled up far enough to clear the hatchway, it swung a distance of seven or eight feet through the water, pushing the Saint ahead of it.

And as he came through the water and

clear of the rail on the side of the sunken boat which had been blind to him while he was working, he saw a sight that made his scalp tingle electrically with the march of ghostly insects, and his heart almost stopped as if a cold hand had clutched it.

There, facing him, anchored to the sea bed close up against the side of the boat, was the answer to the question which had been echoing in his brain: *Where was Bernadotti?*

The man's black hair waved lazily in the currents set up by the swing of the loaded net, and his eyes bulged in the rigid stare of death.

3

"Come on, come on, wake up!" shouted Inspector Lebec impatiently.

Captain William Finnegan began to stir uneasily out of his deep dream of peace; and then someone sloshed another bucketful of cold sea-water over him, none too gently.

Finnegan, flat on his back on the deck of the *Phoenix*, twitched three or four times, then spluttered, gasped, coughed, and finally opened his eyes. He looked up at the impassive form of Lebec framed against the fading blue and white of the evening sky.

"Wha—?" said Finnegan, and shut his eyes again.

Another bucket of water sloshed over him.

"Wha—?" said Finnegan, more loudly.

He tried to get up on one elbow, but fell back.

"Come on—wake up!" Lebec repeated.

Arabella shook her head dubiously.

"What's the use? He couldn't have done it," she said. "Not in that condition."

Lebec stood for a while, chewing his lower lip reflectively as he looked down at the groggily blinking Finnegan. Then he seemed to make up his mind.

"I agree. It is difficult to imagine that he could be capable of anything but sleep. And his condition was no better when we discovered him earlier, in the storage room." Lebec glanced at his watch. "The next load will soon be due. Once we have dealt with it, we will lock him away until he becomes sober."

Arabella looked around at the gold that lay spread out in shallow stacks on the deck. She could still hardly believe it all. It seemed incredible that in the space of two and a half days she could have been through so many experiences of a kind that had never touched her life before. She had been rescued from death in a bull-ring; she had been chased through a swamp and charged with a lance; she had been threatened by grotesquely dice-helmeted characters in a night club and had a man murdered almost in her arms, had been locked up in a police cell, and finally run down by her own yacht. It was quite incredible that all these things had actually happened to her; and it was equally hard to believe in the reality of all that gold.

But there it was before her eyes, gleaming in the rays of the setting sun—the magical sight of real gold in the gold of the sunset. There would be four million dollars' worth, or so, and Lebec had told her that the ten percent reward would go half to her and half to the Saint.

Arabella had to confess to herself that the division seemed more than fair to her. True, without her yacht the gold wouldn't have been found, and her equipment was being used to recover it. But she could hardly forget that it was her husband who had stolen it in the first place; and more than once since Lebec's mention of the reward she had wondered whether as the thief's widow she could not be debarred from taking a share in it.

"How many loads more?" she asked Lebec.

"Your friend Monsieur Templar thought two. One is due now. Then it will be the last."

She indicated the gold on the deck.

"How much so far?"

Lebec fired off the question in French at the crewman from the launch, who was sitting lugubriously by the spare winch they had been using. He was waiting now for the next twitch on the rope, like a bored fisherman waiting for a bite. He consulted the careful record he had been keeping as he and Lebec counted the gold aboard.

"*Cent soixante-cinq*," he said, without turning his head.

"One hundred and sixty-five," Lebec translated. "So, we shall have perhaps two hundred bars, a weight of two thousand kilograms."

Presently there was a tug on the line, and the lugubrious crewman started the winch to haul the penultimate load up and aboard.

"Monsieur Templar has done well," Lebec conceded. "It is hard work, I think."

Simon Templar would have been the first to agree. All the long afternoon he had laboured steadily on the sea bed, loading the gold into the net, bar by bar, jerking the rope each time he had filled and secured it, gradually emptying the boat of its weighty treasure. Four times he had surfaced—once, after the first loading, to report the discovery of Bernadotti's anchored corpse, and three times to renew the air cylinders on his back. And then he had gone down one more time into the deepening green silence, for the last consignment of ingots he intended to send up. The bottom layer he had decided to leave where it was, all for himself, to be collected at some future date.

He glanced at his air gauge as the net came down on its last trip. Fifteen minutes left. It would be enough, and with several minutes to spare. He steered the net into the cabin and began loading.

The discovery of a thoroughly irrigated Bernadotti had unquestionably solved the immediate mystery of his whereabouts, but the other questions still crowded Simon's mind. The enigma of Finnegan was deeper than ever, with things looking blacker for him, by the Saint's previous reasoning. Except that it was all somehow lacking in neatness; it had the untidiness of a theory which the facts would only fit if they were wrenched into shape with Procrustean efforts. And there was now one other loose scrap of fact which suddenly exploded into his consciousness.

Bernadotti's body had manifestly been anchored where it was by someone; and that led by ineluctable logic to the conclusion that there must be another diver somewhere, or at least there must *have been* another diver.

And that deduction reminded him of something which had only half-registered on his attention when he was getting the one remaining scuba outfit from the store-room to being the work of the afternoon.

That was it. The *one* remaining scuba outfit. There had originally been three—the Saint was sure of that. And one, or most of one, had been lost in the incident with the dinghy.

When he had surfaced that afternoon for the first time, he had gone to the store-room and checked again. There was definitely and positively no sign of the third scuba outfit; and although he had not previously counted the spare air tanks he was fairly certain that some of them, too, had gone.

Not being a believer in the ability of diving gear to grow little legs and wander off on its own, any more than in that of corpses to tie themselves to the sea bed, Simon was obliged to believe, by the logic aforesaid, that somebody must have removed the scuba equipment and used it while conveying Bernadotti's body down to its watery burial place.

Which meant, the same logic went on to tell him, that somewhere somebody must still be at large, lurking and hiding, with the gold still his objective.

So they would need to have all their wits about them when they were back on the *Phoenix*.

Who was the *Somebody?* Simon's thoughts swung back to Finnegan. If the mystery of how he might have come to be locked in the store-room could be allowed to pass for the moment—and Simon decided that for the sake of making some mental headway it could—then all the rest was not quite impossible, even including the trick of taking Bernadotti's body down to the bottom of the sea.

The Saint went over the events which had followed on that unguarded moment when the dinghy had been capsized. He pictured it all vividly, in a kind of action replay, with an imaginary stopwatch going in the background. First the collision; then the short period, a minute perhaps, when they had bobbed up and down in the sea, watching the *Phoenix* plough on; then the brief swim; then the pickup by Lebec in the launch; the hauling aboard of Descartes' mangled body; and finally the warily circuitous approach to the *Phoenix*, where she lay at anchor near the sunken boat. In all, perhaps fifteen minutes—twenty at the outside. That could have been enough. Finnegan could have slung the body of Bernadotti overboard, suitably weighted; he could have followed it down, secured it beside the boat, and got back on board and out of his diving gear—all within ten or twelve minutes.

Finnegan could have done it—in theory. The case against him might have been strengthened, but it remained unproved. One point in his favour, although a small point, was that the third set of scuba gear hadn't been found on board. The Captain might yet turn out to be an innocently genuine toper.

In which case, the continuing logic told Simon, there must be someone else at large with the diving gear—perhaps lurking about underwater somewhere nearby.

Simon continued to chew it over as he completed the loading of the net. He gazed up for a moment through the deepening emerald gloom to where the pale underbellies of the two boats hung down below the surface. Nearest him, the *Phoenix*'s big white keel projected down perhaps ten feet, and on the far side of her the much smaller shape of the coastguard launch was tucked in close beside it like a small daughter whale sheltering in her cetacean mother's lee. There was just one place in the immediate area of the two vessels where a diver could feasibly be hiding, or have stayed hidden for any length of time. On the far side of the launch there was a narrow wedge of water, extending a few feet down from the surface, that was invisible both from the Saint's viewpoint on the sea bed, and also from the decks of the *Phoenix;* and that was where Simon intended to look before he finally surfaced.

He had already made a careful inspection all around the sunken wreck itself, with his fingers alert on the hilt of the knife tucked into his weightbelt. He had not seriously expected to find anyone lurking there, figuring that the enemy, whoever that was, would not make his move until the gold had all been loaded aboard.

Therefore the Saint had shelved the problem of the diver, and where he might be concealed, and had simply got on with doing what had to be done. The diver might have gone ashore—the nearest point of land being no more than a hundred yards off— or, as Simon had now realised, he just might be skulking on the blind side of the launch.

The Saint glanced at his air gauge again as he secured the net and tugged on the rope for the last load to be hauled up. He had five minutes left, perhaps six; and that would be enough. Enough to close the hatch, and to investigate that wedge of blind water on his way up.

It was not the first time that Simon Templar had underestimated the opposition; nor was it the first time his calculating of an opponent's next move had been incomplete in some small but potentially disastrous particular. He had reasoned that the enemy would make his move only after the gold had been secured; but he should have realised that the enemy could make up his own mind about when enough gold for his plans had been hauled up.

Of course, when it was all over, it was absurdly obvious. But when foresight was needed, he had missed it.

He had not seen the other diver who slid

silently along the sea bed from the shore a few minutes before; neither did he see that diver now, emerging from a thicket of the viridescent weed nearby to take up silent station by the sunken boat's stern, as the Saint steadied the load from deep inside.

Simon saw the laden net clear the hatchway above him; he saw it swing to one side, as each load before it had done; he saw it begin to recede upwards, off-centre in the greenish rectangle of light framed by the hatchway. And then he saw, with a dumbstruck horror such as he had seldom known in his life before, that rectangle of light suddenly shrink and narrow to a slit, and then to nothing, as the hatch was closed on him from above.

— 4 —

In the Stygian blackness of his underwater dungeon, Simon Templar heard the sound that must surely seal his fate. He heard the grinding and scraping of the heavy locking mechanism as someone secured the hatch above him; and in that instant he could hardly avoid the conviction that destiny must surely have come to claim him at last.

Death had started towards him often enough before, and perhaps half a dozen times had come close enough for him to have felt that his chances of survival were worse than even. But somehow, by a happy combination of luck and resourcefulness, he had always won through, even in circumstances where his prospects looked about as good as those of a three-legged donkey in the Grand National. But never until now had he had to give himself up for dead. On those other occasions, he had always had some reserve of his own, however tenuous, which he might somehow press into service, or some human support in the background to give at least a glimmer of hope; but this time he could think of nothing that would ever get him out.

In the first few seconds, as he realised with that sickening numbness what had happened and would happen yet, he tried, with the desperate strength of three men, to force open the locked hatch. But the attempt was useless. There was nothing for him to brace himself against while he kicked at the hatch, and he could get no real power behind the effort against the resistance of the water.

Perhaps it had been written in the stars, from the very beginning, that this was where his life was to end. He had long known that he could not go on blithely cheating death for ever and a day. That was in the nature of his hazardous trade, which he had chosen freely; and if his nemesis had caught up with him at last, he had no right now to bewail his lot. He had played the game gladly, and won gladly; and now, he had lost. It was as simple as that. There at the bottom of the sea he was alone with his ultimate fate, with not the remotest prospect of the cavalry appearing over the hill at the last minute . . . nor of any other miracle.

In real life there were no miracles; and real life for the Saint had dwindled down into perhaps two hundred cubic feet of underwater blackness, and a couple of minutes of breathing before his air ran out. And then the cabin would become his water tomb, and he would pass out of the living legend and into the historic. And so there was nothing left but to resign himself to the inevitable.

Above the hull, the other diver had continued swiftly and decisively with the execution of his plan. Silently, he surfaced in the blind water on the far side of the launch. He climbed aboard and released an extra

273

length of the boat's anchor rope. He dived again, following the rope to the anchor itself. He dragged it along the sea bed, passed the rope twice around the rail of the sunken cruiser, and then silently swam back to surface again beside the launch. Lebec, Arabella, and the crewmen were busy unloading the gold on to the *Phoenix*'s deck; there was no reason for them to turn to the launch, and they did not see the diver stealthily setting fire to the cushions in its cabin, before he silently slipped back into and under the water.

A minute or so later Lebec suddenly stood still and sniffed the air like a pointer dog. He turned towards the source of the acrid smoke.

"My ship! *Vite!*" he bellowed.

He grabbed a bucket and leapt across to the launch. The crewman followed with a second bucket, and after a momentary hesitation Arabella joined them.

While they were preoccupied with trying to douse the flames, the diver resurfaced between the two boats to proceed to the next stage of his plan. He cut the rope with which Lebec had tied the launch close up to the *Phoenix*. Then he braced himself against the bigger boat, and with his feet he

274

pushed the launch well clear. He boarded the *Phoenix*, and made for the wheelhouse.

Lebec felt the movement of the launch, shouted, then turned in rage and astonishment as the *Phoenix*'s engines came to throbbing life. And the *Phoenix* began to pull away, with someone visible at the wheel who, from that distance, could be recognisable only as a man wearing a diver's wetsuit and mask.

"Templar!" Lebec roared. "Stop! As a police officer I command you to stop!"

The error was pardonable, as Lebec had no way of knowing that the Saint was still at the bottom of the sea.

The seat cushions on the launch were still smouldering, but the fire had done no serious damage. Lebec barked a new order at his crewman; and as the man complied the diesel engines of the launch awoke to drumming life.

"*Allez! Vite!*" Lebec snapped, stabbing an outraged finger in the direction of the *Phoenix* as she headed for the open sea. "After him! Templar shall *not* get away with the gold!"

He flung himself on the anchor cable and hauled. At first the rope began to come easily aboard as Lebec took up the slack;

then the rope tautened, stretched, and held fast.

With a string of Gallic profanities Lebec shouted another order. The man said something back, and Lebec took over the helm and opened the throttle. The launch's propeller churned the water into a froth; and its nose tilted up as it strained against the creaking wet rope that tethered it. But it remained tethered; and the enraged Lebec frantically piled on more power as he watched the *Phoenix* heading out to sea.

Down below, in what he had accepted would soon become his sodden sepulchre, Simon Templar had heard the last hiss of air released by his tanks. Then there was nothing left but to re-breathe what remained in the tubes and in his face mask.

A stubborn instinctive will to live compelled him to try to make it last as long as possible by controlled shallow breathing, even though common sense told him that it could only postpone oblivion by a few futile minutes.

His ribs ached, and a kind of merciful red mist came up before his eyes to distance him from what was happening in the final seconds . . .

As the red mist darkened, somewhere above him a man at the helm of a boat switched to reverse gear and crammed on full power again, and held the throttle wide open while the turbulent water boiled around the boat with a frustrated churning of the screws, and a suffocating fog of diesel fumes engulfed it.

Simon Templar did not hear the straining of the stretched anchor rope, nor the slow sucking and splintering and rending sound made by the rotten timbers of the sunken wreck as the sustained traction on the teth-ered cable pulled it apart. Nor was he con-scious enough to see clearly the gaping aperture of greenish light that opened up like a heaven above his head as the stern-rail and a torn-off section of deck were dragged slowly upward. It could only have been by blind reflexes that he groped his way out and up towards that light, strengthened by some reawakened spark of hope which had defiantly survived in him.

And then, as he broke surface, the feel of air on his skin must have brought conscious-ness briefly back to him. At any rate, some-thing told him to tear off his face mask and take two great gulping gasping breaths, as hands reached down from the launch to bring him aboard, before the mist came up in front of his eyes again and became an infinite and engulfing black void.

VII: How there was a Three-way Reunion, and the Saint saw more Fun Ahead.

—1—

Simon Templar opened his eyes again in tentative incredulity, to regard the back of Inspector Gérard Lebec's head. Objectively speaking it was nothing remarkable, as the backs of heads went; but to the Saint it was indubitably one of the most beautiful sights he had ever seen.

He shifted his glance, and met the blue gaze and concerned expression of Arabella Tatenor. He was lying across two of the seats in the cabin of the launch, with his head resting in her lap; and the Saint had never before felt so utterly amazed and overwhelmed to be alive.

The gold on the deck of the fleeing *Phoenix* was for that moment a dream forgotten as completely as if it had never been. Even the world that impinged directly on his senses had the lambent quality of a fantasy; and he looked around him with a fresh-eyed wonderment. It was the unbelievable fantasy of a world which he had just given up as irrevocably lost. Never before had life seemed so overflowing with the sensory riches of the moving present that was now, and never before had the seed of that present seemed to hold such an infinite burgeoning of promise for the future. Just to be alive was a fabulous wine of contentment, and at that moment he wanted nothing more than to remain utterly immersed in it.

He hooked an arm up slowly behind Arabella's red-gold head and drew her down gently for a kiss. And this too was an astonishment and a fantasy—this woman, ripe and beautiful and tender, who gave herself willingly to his kiss, and returned it . . .

And then abruptly, almost with an audible click, he was fully back in life again. The sky and the sea and Arabella and Lebec and the man at the helm of the launch somersaulted dizzily back into their familiar perspective in the real world; and now it was the last place he had been to, on the murky margins of annihilation that was the fantasy, fading into a blurred and receding memory of life surrendering to death.

Then, with that return of his normal mind, he thought of the man who had locked him up under the sea—the man who had slammed down and secured the hatch and left him down there alone to suffocate and die in the darkness. And if ever iron entered into a man's soul, it entered into the soul of Simon Templar then.

There was no justice he could imagine subscribing to which would not make the perpetrator of that action pay for it in the very same coin—the coin of life. For the Saint, there could be no other possible price, and no other acceptable executioner but himself; and he knew that, whatever else might happen, he would do everything in his power to carry out the sentence, and that when the time came he would do it unflinchingly and without compunction.

Now he gazed forward across the sea, and saw the *Phoenix* ahead against the pink glow on the western horizon where the sun had gone down not long before. The *Phoenix* had perhaps four hundred yards on them, and the launch was closing the gap fast.

Lebec turned to him.

"So you have recovered, Monsieur Templar. Are you able to tell us—who is the diver? Who is that man driving the *Phoenix?*"

Simon's eyes were chips of frozen sapphire as he thought of that driver—that man.

"I don't know," he said quietly. "But I mean to find out, just as soon as you can catch up and get this tub close enough for me to jump on board."

While the launch steadily ate up the *Phoenix*'s lead, Simon sketched in the bare essentials of what had happened in those final few minutes on the sea bed. Lebec listened attentively, his pale green eyes appraising the Saint's lean and dangerous form; and he must have drawn his own conclusions from what he saw.

Perhaps the hard-set fighting line of the Saint's mouth and the flinty resolution in his eyes made his intentions only too plain. Not that he had made any special attempt to conceal them. But at any rate, Lebec abruptly drew his automatic with the air of a man who had made up his mind about a point which had been worrying him.

"Monsieur Templar," he said, "you will not be permitted to step on to the *Phoenix* until after *I* have dealt with this man. You will remain here—and Madame also, for her own safety."

At a word from Lebec the crewman drew his own gun and pointed it at the Saint. And Simon was glumly obliged to admit its controlling power, and to remain where he was while the launch drew level with the *Phoenix*'s port quarter.

The crewman manoeuvred the launch close in, and Lebec stood up on the rail to make the short jump across the after deck. And in that instant the Saint knew that, come what might, this was one party he couldn't bear to miss.

There was no way that he could sit there among the charred cushions in the cabin of the coastguard launch while Lebec followed formal police procedure to bring the man at the helm of the *Phoenix* into the custody and protection of the law, with all the asininely bureaucratic due processes which that implied. As soon as he saw Lebec on board the *Phoenix*, with automatic in hand, he realised that he had to take action immediately if he was to have any hope of substituting Saintly retributive justice for those due processes.

There was only one thing to be done, and he did it. It involved elements of risk; but what was that after what he had already come through?

He took the two easy unhurried strides that were needed to bring him within easy range of the crewman at the helm, and he took them as if it had been the most natural thing in the world to approach for a chat; and that was the first risk taken. The crewman might have had a twitchy trigger finger, easily set off by any threatening movement on the Saint's part; but Simon had studied his lugubrious features and his generally slow and deliberate behaviour, and gambled that the man was the opposite of twitchy; and the gamble had come off.

The next stage of the operation demanded a quick burst of the brilliant acting which the Saint could turn on like a tap when the need arose. As he reached the armed crewman, after those two relaxed strides across the cabin, he began to speak, in French, in a friendly conversational tone that exactly fitted the pace of his casual steps.

"*Il a beaucoup de courage, votre chef,*" he began; but he interrupted himself abruptly by turning his head sharply towards the *Phoenix* as if he had suddenly seen something that took his breath away.

"*Mon Dieu!*" he gasped; and the crewman looked off in the same direction.

He would hardly have been human if he had not turned his own head in response to Simon's totally convincing diversion; and the Saint truly regretted that the exigencies of the situation called for the crewman to suffer a little bodily harm. That regret, however, could not be allowed to weaken his resolve. His left hand shot out like a greased piston, and his fingers closed over the man's gun wrist; and almost at the same instant his right fist, travelling about eighteen inches through the air in a scorching uppercut, impacted with bone-jarring force under the man's mournful jaw.

The crewman crumpled with scarcely a sound, and Simon caught him and let him gently down. Then he picked up the gun and toyed with it in momentary hesitation.

"Another old trick?" Arabella enquired; and Simon nodded.

The old light of battle was in his eyes as he handed her the gun. What he had to do, he would do with his bare hands.

"Wave it at him if he wakes up," he said. "Tell him you'll shoot if he comes closer than five feet—and sound as if you mean it!"

And then he was gone, his feet taking him noiselessly on to the rail and then across to the *Phoenix* through the gathering dusk; and Arabella sat looking from the gun in her hand to the unconscious crewman, and back to the gun.

Lebec had perhaps a minute's start on

him; and the Saint had no very clear plan of what to do next. It was one of those situations where, as so often before, he simply followed his impulse and instinct. All he knew was that he was back in the game, with Lebec ahead of him, and the man in the wheelhouse an unknown quantity—though the Saint had his suspicions on that score . . .

He had been over his speculations about Tranchier's survival often enough by this time; and he was not unprepared for the sound that reached his ears as he glided along the deck of the *Phoenix* towards the wheelhouse like a liquid shadow.

He heard two voices speaking in rapid French, one of them Lebec's; and he flattened himself against a bulkhead where he could not be seen from the door of the wheelhouse or its companionway. And as he listened, his eyes widened with steadily growing comprehension.

"Will you or will you not surrender?" Lebec's voice demanded from what the Saint judged to be somewhere near the foot of the companionway.

"You'll have to shoot me first," said the other man, from higher up.

There was a pause; then Lebec said:

"If I must, I will shoot you. There will be no witnesses. Templar and the woman are on the launch with the coastguard man. I will say it was self-defence, that you resisted arrest. And so after all the gold will be mine alone, and you will have gained nothing by your death."

"But you will still have the problem of those three—and Finnegan—to deal with, alone." A faintly crafty note crept into the other voice. "Gérard—why don't we make a deal? There's more than enough for two. We could throw the four bodies overboard, set the launch adrift, and get clean away."

There was another pause; and while Lebec was thinking, so was the Saint. For the dialogue he had overheard gave him all he needed to think about.

First, there was Lebec's clear and unpolicemanlike desire to grab the gold for himself. Second, there was the fact that the other man had called him "Gérard" in a way that implied an intimate acquaintance. Thirdly, there was the man's voice.

Simon had never, that he could remember, heard Tranchier-Fournier speak; and yet there was something in the tone of that other Frenchman in the *Phoenix*'s wheelhouse, a confidence and authority, even an arrogance, which didn't fit the impression he had formed of Tranchier.

Then it hit him like a sudden blast of arctic air; and in that instant of amazed realisation, as the pieces of the puzzle began to click into precise place, he stepped out from behind the bulkhead and into view.

He saw Inspector Gérard Lebec, standing only part-way up the companionway, swinging around in alarm. And in the doorway at the top, facing him, he saw the other man— a man with a big square head, grey-white hair, and suntanned features.

It could only be Karl Schwarzkopf, also known as Charles Tatenor.

—— 2 ——————————————

"*Salut Karl!*" said the Saint in a voice of steel-lined velvet.

Even though he had come out into the open without premeditation, simply because he had had to confirm Schwarzkopf as the owner of the second voice as soon as the fantastic conviction had come to him, Simon's reflexes were immediately balanced on a razor edge. He was acutely aware of being unarmed, and that the reaction of

Lebec, with his automatic, was unpredictable.

Lebec was certainly taken by surprise; and his adjustment to the Saint's abrupt arrival on the scene was perhaps half a second slower than Schwarzkopf's.

Which was unfortunate for Lebec.

As the French detective swung his head, followed by his gun arm, away from Schwarzkopf and towards Simon, Schwarzkopf moved—and with amazing speed. He launched himself down the companionway at Lebec feet-first, with a force that should have sent him cannoning into the Saint. But Simon's reactions were also fast, and he side-stepped. Lebec made the close and violent acquaintance of a bulkhead, and sank to the deck with all the wind knocked out of him. Somehow he managed to hold on to the automatic, but it was two or three seconds before he could collect his breath and his wits to use it.

Two or three seconds was all Schwarzkopf needed. He must have summed up the situation to himself—including Simon's own lack of a visible weapon—in the instant of launching himself at Lebec; and now, as Lebec lay gasping on the deck, Schwarzkopf leapt back up the companionway, snatched up a Very pistol in the wheelhouse, and reappeared in the doorway.

And as Lebec brought his automatic up again, Schwarzkopf fired.

The Saint had seen weird deaths before, but this was a sight to persist in his memory for many long years. That brilliant dazzling flare was like a photographic flashbulb fixing the image in the mind. In its vivid and garish light, Lebec's amazed expression was thrown into stark and unforgettable relief. The flare hit him, so to speak, amidships, sank deeply into his torso, and continued to blaze brilliantly as the stricken Lebec emitted a bloodcurdling scream, staggered backward to the rail, and crashed over it and into the sea.

Both Schwarzkopf and the Saint watched Lebec's final disappearance in frozen fascination for the few seconds it occupied. And then Schwarzkopf, still gripping the signal-pistol, whirled, and disappeared back into the wheelhouse. The Saint had to make an immediate choice, either to conceal himself—playing hide-and-seek with an armed man—or to go forward and try to get to Schwarzkopf before he could reload the pistol.

He went forward.

With one long stride he was at the foot of the companionway, and with two more co-ordinated thrusts of arms and legs he was at the top and into the wheelhouse doorway.

He had never climbed a companionway faster; but as he reached the doorway he knew he had not been fast enough. Schwarzkopf had just finished thrusting a new flare into the Very pistol. He levelled it at the Saint, and the Saint came to a slow halt in the doorway.

So this was how the game was to end, after all, he thought; and there was a certain inescapable bitterness in the reflection that he had survived, by one of those miracles he had thought impossible, this man's earlier attempt to kill him, only to find himself now facing death once more at the same hand—the hand of Karl Schwarzkopf, the only survivor of a boat crash which had killed, not "Tatenor" and Tranchier, and not "Tatenor" alone, but Tranchier alone.

For it was "Tatenor", the man Schwarz-kopf, now standing before him and about to pull the trigger of the signal-pistol for the second time, who was the clever one. Why should the relatively stupid Tranchier have been able to worst him and escape to claim the gold for himself? Simon could see it all now; but he could also see why he had been backing the wrong horse as the survivor. Karl Schwarzkopf, whose attention to detail had been impeccable, was the survivor now . . .

Except that the expected shot had still not come.

Schwarzkopf motioned with the Very pistol.

"So—Templar. Where's the rest of the gold, old chap?" he said in his measured and hauntingly overprecise English. "What did you do with it, eh?"

So that was it. Only the other man's avarice had prolonged Simon's life even that long.

"How do you mean—the *rest* of the gold?" the Saint queried, apparently in genuine puzzlement.

"Come, come now." Schwarzkopf-Tatenor made an impatient movement with the pistol. "You've already caused me more than enough trouble with your confounded interference. Let's not waste time. You may have very little of it remaining. Let's be sensible. You know I'm not a fool, and I pay you the compliment of acknowledging that you're not weak in the head either. I've seen the tally of the gold on deck, I know how many bars were down there on the sea bed originally, and I know how many I've removed over the years. It's a matter of simple arithmetic. Forty-one are left unaccounted for. You must have moved them. I want to know where they are."

"They're somewhere you'll never find them," the Saint said.

The other smiled mirthlessly.

"I'll give you a minute or two to reconsider," he said—and the Saint heard again that note of cunning which he had heard while he listened to Schwarzkopf's conversation with Lebec. "Perhaps we can come to some arrangement. As matters stand at the moment, those forty-one bars of gold are lost to me. If you will tell me where they are or better, accompany me to recover them I'd be prepared to share them with you. So you would emerge with something for your pains, and also with your life."

The Saint shook his head sadly.

"Karl, you're beginning to disappoint me. Just now you were prepared to give me credit for being slightly less than an idiot. Now you're throwing me a bait no self-respecting half-wit would take. No deal, Karl. You're much too smart to leave me alive—now that I know you're alive."

Schwarzkopf gazed intently at him, but said nothing; and Simon continued.

"Yes, Karl, you always were a clever fellow, weren't you? *Ein geschickter Kerl.* Brilliant scholar and linguist, high flyer with the bank in Paris. And when your partners in crime were unclever enough to get caught, you were bright enough to take off with the loot—and to get away with it."

"Why should I pay for their stupidity?" Schwarzkopf said calmly. "They wanted their champagne, the imbeciles. Well, they had it. And I had the gold."

"And then," Simon went on, "you perfected your new identity—the upper-crust sporting Englishman. And you did it brilliantly enough to fool everyone . . . Until fish-features Tranchier turned up; and he wouldn't go away, would he? What a pain he must have been to you, Karl! You couldn't even have bought him off, because Descartes and the others would have been down on you before long. There was only one way out for you; and that was to die, or appear to die. And since Fish-face was sticking so close to you, it had to be done in a way that either convinced him or got rid of him permanently along with 'Tatenor'."

Schwarzkopf smiled that curiously mirthless smile again, but there was a hint of pride in his face too.

"It was a brilliant solution, wasn't it? To kill the man Tatenor—so that the others would cease looking for him—for me."

"Yes, Karl, it was a great idea," the Saint agreed. "And who was the other man in the boat—the other body? Some poor down-and-out you clobbered? Or a solitary tourist on the island who wasn't likely to be missed at home for a week or two? And next, I suppose, you'd have surfaced in France, or back in Switzerland, or somewhere else, with another new identity, leaving your widow with nothing. Yes, it was clever all right. As I said, you're a brainy fellow."

"So I'm brainy enough to know when I should make a deal," Schwarzkopf said in level tones.

"And I know that your name is Schwarzkopf, not *Dummkopf*. Any deal with me would mean no more than the one you tried to make with Lebec. You had to try something there, because he had a gun on you. With me, you're trying it on because you think I might be able to tell you where there's more gold; and you're greedy for it all. But eventually you'd kill me anyway, like you killed Lebec . . . By the way, he *was* the sixth man, I suppose? You called him 'Gérard'."

"He was our partner at the Moroccan end of the operation," Schwarzkopf said. "I expect he joined the Marseille police in order to remain in the area where he presumed the gold might still be hidden. He seems to have been obsessed with it."

"But he had to die, didn't he—once he knew what you were up to? And the same applies to me, and the others. You can't afford to leave anyone alive who knows about the gold. You'll have to kill me, and you'll have to kill the coastguard man." The Saint paused, and then added with an inexorable finality in his voice: "And then, Karl, you're going to have to kill your own wife. How easy will you find that? *Wirdst du selbst deine eigene Frau umbringen können?*"

Simon could see that the last thrust had gone home. The need to face the problem of Arabella must have been the only thing that could give a pang to Schwarzkopf's case-hardened conscience. The Saint, as the person who had relentlessly brought him face to face with that last shocking question, became the object and the focus of the anger that now erupted through the surface of Schwarzkopf's polished self-command; and with the final question fired at him in German, which was after all the language nearest to his own, the man's linguistic control had been broken down too. He answered in a German rapidly devolving into his own guttural Swiss dialect.

"Ja! Du hesch rächt!" he snarled, holding the pistol pointed rigidly. *"Meine Frau muss ich gleichfalls umbringen. Aber jetzt, Templar, itz längts mit dr Imischig. Itz lani di abe, du Soucheib!"*

Simon Templar did not understand every word Tatenor had said in that peculiar honkingly guttural accent; but the sense was as clear as day, and more urgent. And now, as Schwarzkopf's finger tightened visibly on the trigger of the Very pistol, Simon knew that evasive action was his only slim hope of escaping the spectacular fate of Lebec.

The timing had to be perfect, and the flare not too low; and all the Saint could do was to concentrate his profound and undeviating attention on the former, watching that trigger-knuckle as it whitened, for the fraction of a second during which it moved. He judged the distance, and then . . .

To say that he ducked would be absurdly inadequate. He dropped. Or perhaps he half-dropped and half-dived down on to the companionway; and the flare swooshed over his head and out to sea.

And then he felt an urgent tug at his ankle; and he looked down and saw Arabella, holding the crewman's automatic out to him in mute and terrible decision.

He dropped vertically the remaining few feet down the side of the companionway. Their eyes met briefly in silence, and he took the gun. They could hear the sounds of reloading in the wheelhouse, and a second or two later Schwarzkopf reappeared in the doorway.

And before he could fire the signal-pistol for the third time, Simon Templar shot him through the heart.

3

"And then," said the Saint the next morning, "there was a nice touch of detail, a little bit of special care on his part, that had me fooled and sniffing off on the wrong scent. You remember I said I'd made some enquiries at the station? Well, the sharp-eyed little stationmaster said the stranger who'd travelled without bags had a French accent.

I was already thinking of Tranchier, and that about clinched it in my mind. But Charles—Karl—was so smart he'd anticipated the possibility that someone might be suspicious about the boat crash, and nosey enough to make enquiries—and he prepared the ground so that, if anyone was suspected of having survived it, that someone would be Tranchier. He was certainly thorough, your Charles."

Arabella turned over on her towel and looked around at the gold that still lay stacked on the deck of the *Phoenix*.

"Thorough enough to have killed me too." She turned to face Simon: "It's lucky I heard him say so—lucky I could understand enough German for that. Otherwise I could never have given you the gun—you know that?"

"Yes," said the Saint. "I know. And you know now that I wasn't the sixth man. Lebec was. All those years in the police, he must have been waiting, and wondering if he'd ever hear of that gold. He must have known about Descartes and the others, of course. He'd probably been watching them since they first arrived in the village. And then we turned up, and led him straight to the hoard—and to his old accomplice Karl."

"And it was Charles—Karl—who tried to kill you in the night club, and who drove the van. And later, he must have been hiding on the *Phoenix* all the time."

Simon nodded.

"Except when Lebec and I searched the ship."

"And where was he then?"

"He could have been underwater, lurking on the blind side of the launch. But my guess is that he headed for the shore at the nearest point. It was only about a hundred yards from where we were, and there are some big rocks there. He'd have kept behind them out of sight until it was time to move. He could probably hear what I shouted to Lebec from the water, or anyway enough of it to know when I was getting near the end of the job."

Arabella pondered for a while longer. Then she said:

"What about all this gold, Simon?"

"We're returning it to the authorities, of course," he said virtuously. "And claiming the reward."

The coastguard cutter was keeping level with the *Phoenix*, about fifty yards off the starboard beam, escorting them watchfully back to Marseille.

"And how about the coastguard—won't he make a fuss about being slugged?"

Simon stretched lazily in the sun.

"I squared it with him. I apologised handsomely—and sincerely. I explained that Lebec was a rotten egg. The crewman'll get a tenth of our ten percent—I mean a fifth of my five percent."

"And if the Marseilles police aren't satisfied about Lebec's death?" she persisted.

"They will be—once they dig into his past in Morocco and find the connections with the bullion job."

Arabella pondered a while longer.

"And Finnegan? He was always just what he seemed, then?" she said finally.

"Innocent as a tipsy lamb," Simon agreed. "And he's back in top form." He indicated the ship's wake stretching away to the southeast behind them in a series of broad zigzags. "However, if I were you, I'd think twice about keeping him on as captain."

Something else occurred to Arabella.

"Simon," she said slowly, as she traced the line of his tanned shoulder with a finger. "It looks as though you're not going to be left with so much out of all this. Four percent. Isn't that an awfully small commission—for the Saint?"

301

He grinned, and ruffled her hair where the sun glinted on the red and gold of it.

"Well, to tell you the truth," he said. "I did manage to keep a bit of the gold back. Forty-one bars, to be precise. Somehow I just forgot to send them up."

Arabella gazed at him in wonder, and then she threw back her head and chuckled with abandoned delight.

"So you've left half a million dollars down there! . . . But wait a minute. We pulled up part of the boat, remember? The whole thing may have been moved, dragged along the sea bed. Will you be able to find it again?"

"I think so," said the Saint. "At any rate, I'm going to have a lot of fun trying."

"We certainly are," said Arabella.

The publishers hope that this
Large Print Book has brought
you pleasurable reading.
Each title is designed to make
the text as easy to see as possible.
G.K. Hall Large Print Books
are available from your library and
your local bookstore. Or, you can
receive information by mail on
upcoming and current Large Print Books
and order directly from the publishers.
Just send your name and address to:

G.K. Hall & Co.
70 Lincoln Street
Boston, Mass. 02111

or call, toll-free:

1-800-343-2806

A note on the text
Large print edition designed by
Bernadette Montalvo.
Composed in 16 pt Plantin
on a Xyvision 300/Linotron 202N
by Stephen Traiger
of G.K. Hall & Co.